THE GRAND TOUR

A JACKSON'S UNREAL CIRCUS & MOBILE
MARMALADE COLLECTION

E. CATHERINE TOBLER

To anyone who ever wanted to run away.

INTRODUCTION

BY A.C. WISE

Have you ever wanted to run away and join the circus?

Are you sure?

The sound of the train chugging into town, cars packed with wonder and mystery and excitement, is also the sound of danger. That first whisper of calliope music is a promise, and also a lie. All circuses are built on illusion—a magical city springing up overnight, unfolded from train cars, poured into tents that bloom from the ground like strange flowers, and populated by familiar strangers beckoning you with reassuring smiles. But nothing in the circus is what it seems. A former nun may really be one of the fates, as old as time itself, endlessly weaving together the lives of those around her while her sisters measure and cut. A simple jar of marmalade may actually contain an entire season, a perfectly preserved memory, or the cure for a broken heart.

Do you still want to run away and join the circus? Are you sure? Jackson's Unreal Circus and Mobile Marmalade is not for the faint of heart, but it rewards those who are brave enough to peer into its shadows and forsake safety for the unknown. You, yes you there, you look like one of the brave ones. Step right up, and have a look inside.

In Jackson's Unreal Circus, E. Catherine Tobler has created a world where time is slippery, where readers may touch down in 1936 in New Orleans, only to be whisked away to Philadelphia in the 1950s, and ultimately land in the Rocky Mountains in 2001. Yet, the circus is also timeless. It is everywhere and everywhen. It is a fantastical place, and it is a deeply human one, full of universal stories threaded with longing, lost love, joy, melancholy, and the strange and unwanted searching for themselves and finding a new home.

It is a world that is both dark and beautiful, simultaneously strange and familiar. If, like me, you grew up on Ray Bradbury, you will find echoes of his classics here, like *Dark Carnival* and *Something Wicked This Way Comes*. And you will also find something that is wholly its own, one hundred percent pure Tobler. Picking up this collection, and delving into its stories, is like setting off on a journey somewhere very far away, and at the same time, it feels like coming home.

In these pages, you will encounter a train, variable in size, containing hidden depths and hidden dimensions. You will find worlds in glass jars of all shapes and colors. Strange dogs. Dangerous men. Conjoined twins with two minds wrapped together in a single skin. You will wander through tales of fantasy, horror, science fiction, and find yourself at the intersection of all three, in a place that defies categorization. These are the delights Jackson's Unreal Circus has in store for you. These, and many more.

The book in your hands is a ticket. To redeem it, all you have to do is turn the page. Be warned, once you do, you will find that Jackson's Unreal Circus is a two-sided coin where sensuality is paired with violence and pain, beauty with sorrow, the calm surface with the unseen dangers that lurks beneath.

You will also enter a world that will take your breath away, prose like a siren-song that will lure you deeper within the maze of train tracks and fairways and tents until you are utterly lost and cannot emerge. Until you find you have no desire to be anywhere but where you are.

Are you ready to run away and join the circus? Of course you are. Because you were always going to say yes to this, danger and all. The moment you heard the train chugging its way toward you, the voice of the barker drifting on the breeze, you had already agreed. The book in your hands is an invitation, one you've been waiting for your entire life. It's okay to be a little scared, and to be excited too. Jackson's Unreal Circus has room for both, it contains multitudes, including wonders crafted just for you.

That's the magic of stories and the circus both, they mean something different to everyone. Every performance is a little different, depending on what the audience brings and how they play their part in the show. You didn't think you were here just to observe, did you? That's not how this circus works. You have to prepared to give a little part of yourself away, but don't worry, you will get so much in return.

So, step right up, come on in. It's time to run away with the circus of your dreams and let it run away with you. Prepare to be amazed.

DESTINATIONS

Vanishing Act
1947, Roswell, New Mexico

Artificial Nocturne
1936, New Orleans, Louisiana

We, as One, Trailing Embers
1911, Coney Island, New York

Liminal
1880, silver rush Colorado

Blow the Moon Out

1957, Philadelphia

Ebb Stung By the Flow
1940, the Trans-Siberian Railway

Lady Marmalade
1946, your hometown

Every Season
2001, the foothills of the Rocky Mountains

Inland Territory, Stray Italian Greyhound
The end of the world

VANISHING ACT

Jackson's Unreal Circus and Mobile Marmalade picked her up a day outside Denver. Jackson wouldn't stop for a cow on the tracks, but he stopped for this little thing, with her pale hair and paler eyes. Brought the entire train to a stop to scoop her from the tracks with his long arms.

She huddled against his chest, her small body nearly folded in on itself, and we all watched, in confusion and fascination both. The long hem of her dirty shift caught the cow catcher and the remains of said beast.

She was none of my concern, but Jackson placed her in my car and made her just that. He lay her down in the corner, in my favorite chair, my only chair. She looked all the more pale against the blue and gold stripes. Their brilliance had long since faded, but looked new against her washed out skin. Her bare feet were crusted with dirt and muck and I didn't look much beyond that.

I was working with the quarters when she began to wail, rolling them across my fingers before trying to turn them into nickels. The steam whistle crowed as we crossed the state line, Colorado into New Mexico, and she came alive as though submerged in hot water.

The quarters tumbled off my fingers, onto the floor where they lay as she shrieked, curled her hands over her ears, and moaned. Her face was creased with pain; for a moment, she looked like she'd been raked with hot metal, so did these creases mark her pale skin.

After listening to her, I wanted to do the same; curl into a ball and moan. Instead, I went to her. Crouched before the chair and tried to get her to lower her hands.

First thing I noticed was that her hands didn't feel like hands. She was soft, as though her bones hadn't yet firmed up. A baby in the guise of a ten year old. Second thing I noticed was the way she went quiet when I touched her.

I thought she would twist away, scream, holler, anything but what she did, which was melt into me, against my chest. Her soft hand curled its way into my shirtfront, her thumb working over the nearest dirty button.

"Stop that."

Tried to push her out of my arms, I did, but she wouldn't go. She took to purring like a cat, like the big lions Jackson kept caged in the car behind mine. To keep me in line, he said, but I could make them vanish with a thought. Still, I didn't like the idea of where they might end up, so I left them alone, and they did the same for me.

The girl's purring took up residence inside my head, worked some kind of magic and made me tumble toward the mattress Opal had snickered at, but had still come to. And where did that memory come from, I wondered as I drowned inside that rumbling sound. I was lost inside it as though it was a maze. Couldn't find my way out, so I just gave in and eventually it bled into a familiar dark quiet I recognized as sleep.

Woke to the train slowing again and I wondered if Jackson was stopping for another sprite on the tracks. Stars painted the sky overhead and the air smelled like manure. We'd reached our destination then.

I untangled myself from the boneless girl. She lay as though dead and I moved away as quick as I could. Before she could latch on again. Before she thought to hold me and purr and make me a lost thing.

The air outside was cool, smelled like snow would be on the ground come morning. I pulled my coat around me, rubbed my hands together, and approached the first of the weird sisters as they emerged from their own car. I offered up one hand; Gemma took it, but Sombra's hand was just as quickly there. It seemed one hand around mine, though I knew there to be two.

The sisters were two halves of the same thing, one light and one dark. Where one was concave, the other was convex. Where one was sharp rocks, the other was smooth water. Sombra's hair was the night sky while Gemma's was the stars. And sometimes, they were exactly backwards from that.

Why, I wondered, couldn't Jackson have placed the little girl in with them? They were women, they'd had children, countless children, or so they said. I'd had plenty of women, but no children. Never would. Didn't need or want them. Would be all too easy to wish them gone and have them vanish.

Sombra and Gemma moved like fog across the ground. Their feet never touched the ground as they drifted away. They wouldn't help with the unloading; they never did and no one ever expected they would. They floated into the night and dissolved into fireflies against the blackness as they swept and blessed the campsite.

Five long and pale fingers wrapped around my half-warmed hand and I started at the touch. Looked down and found the little girl clutching me, her fingers warmed, water barely contained by skin. She looked up at me and her mouth curled in a crescent moon smile.

I could see now that her pale hair was drawn into dread-locks. Messy on the ends like they hadn't been tended in a few years. Her mouth was as pale as her skin; her smile slipped away, but her grip tightened and she looked around, as if to ask where and why we were.

"Performin' here," I said and tried to loose my hand from hers, but she was having none of it. I walked and she fell into easy step beside me, though her little legs shouldn't have been able to keep up.

Silas and Lawrence were already unloading the tents. I finally shook the girl's hand off of mine, swung up into the car, and helped Hunter roll another of the striped cylinders to the door. We maneuvered it around, gave it a swift kick down, and the boys carried it off.

There were twenty-four tents in all. The girl watched me the whole time, perched like an owl on the fence across from the door. Her eyes were almost blue, but as the last tent came down I decided the color was only from the nearest light. She would move away and her eyes would change, no doubt.

"Got a name?" I asked her as I came out of the car and headed back toward mine. She watched me as I took a rumpled cigarette from my coat and placed flame against its tip. Drew deep and exhaled once before she answered.

"You?"

"Ladies first," I insisted. She was tiny and odd, but a lady nonetheless. Her colorless eyes skimmed over me, then met mine again.

"Rabi," she said, and I choked on the smoke that rolled down my throat.

She snatched the cigarette from my hand, tossed it to the ground, and mashed it under her pale toes. I thought I might cough up my stomach, but she brushed her fingers down my arm and I calmed. Instantly, like my mother touching me after a nightmare. I looked at her through the fall of my hair.

"At's *my* name." My voice was hoarse. I turned and thumped the side of my car. Painted in silver by Gemma, trimmed in black by Sombra, was my name and my claim to fame. Rabi, Vanquisher and Vanisher Extraordinaire.

The little girl's mouth twisted and she looked around, searching for another name. Any would do, any name, any word. She looked like a snowflake standing there, eyes flitting from thing to thing, the dirty hem of her shift lifting in the cold breeze. Her skin should have been puckered from the cold, her toes burned from the cigarette, but she showed no discomfort.

Finally, she shook her head.

I shrugged. Didn't matter. She wasn't mine to name. I'd be damned if I was going to do it.

Work continued through the night. The little girl didn't seem to tire; she helped where she thought she could, with small things, and took to following the weird sisters when they returned. She was the reverse of a shadow, but the very shadow Sombra should have had right then; as pale as she was dark. And when it was Gemma's turn to darken, the child could flutter in her wake.

I hauled a rope, helped pull a tent upright. The red and white striped fabric soared against the pre-dawn sky, snapped as the ropes pulled it taut. That cloth shuddered as inner supports were placed thus and so, ribs and organs and muscles to give the beast a chance of standing.

The marmalade stand was up before the sun, which wasn't saying much as snow had begun to fall. Too many clouds for there to be sun. I crossed the stubble grass, drawn by the scent of Beth's fresh rolls and marmalade. I bought a small jar of the orange and a bundle of rolls, kissed her cheek, and let her squeeze my backside before I walked back to my car.

Found the little girl there, wrapped in the blue blanket with its purple stars. She looked like a ghost and I told her as much.

"Not a ghost," she said, and I saw that she had one of my books. I didn't have many. It was the atlas she had spread in her lap, and she pointed to a small town. "We are here."

I nodded as I punched a hole in the bag of rolls. Drew one out, cracked open the jar of marmalade. I tore the roll open next and two fingers sufficed as knife to spread the marmalade. The girl's attention was drawn away from the book; she watched me spread the marmalade, lift, and eat the roll. Marmalade clung to my lips; I licked them clean and she mimicked the motion.

"Gemma says you make things vanish," she said as I finished the roll in three more bites. The rolls were so hot, they'd steamed the bag. I took another one out and tossed it to her. Her watery fingers caught it without hesitation. She broke it open, inhaled the fragrant steam, and stretched her hand toward the marmalade.

Her long fingers were better suited to working as knives. She spread the marmalade smooth and even and took a cautious bite, then another, then made the roll disappear in the cavern of her mouth. With a swallow it was gone.

"You make things vanish," she repeated.

And I knew she didn't mean the roll I'd just eaten. "That's what I do." I nodded and tore open my second roll. She came closer and took another from the bag. She went slower with her second, as I did with mine.

"Really vanish, not magic vanish."

I nodded again, and I never liked where this conversation was going. It was classic, as though she'd pressed her ear against the side of my car a few weeks ago and listened while Anne begged me to do it, to make him vanish and stop beating on her and how could I say no, why wouldn't I do it, couldn't I understand? She wailed—wailed like the girl did when we crossed the state line—and I knew what was coming.

Except it didn't. Not yet.

We sat, in companionable calm, eating rolls and marmalade, while the snow fell silently beyond the open car door.

Ritual and tradition play a big part in Jackson's life and so it was on the first evening that he gathered we performers together. A meal, not lavish, but steaming and generous, had been spread atop the ancient wood table Jackson claimed to have carted from one side of Europe and back again before the war. And at this table we all took our places, under the softly flowing fabric of the big top.

Seeing as how the little girl didn't have a place, she made herself one. A round full moon resting in Sombra's lap, that's how she looked. She didn't help herself to much that night; she took a biscuit and some water, but little else, though Sombra tried to get her interested in the beans. Nope, she was determined not to have any.

I sat between Foster and Jackson, and Jackson seemed genuinely happy about the stay we would have in this little town. These folk were dying for some good entertainment.

Kids had seen the posters, he said, and no matter the dirt and rips, they'd run home. Foster could picture them digging out cans of pennies. They'd be back and he'd be counting those pennies. Foster always smelled like money, like old paper and metal.

Denver had been good to us, but this little place would be better. New Mexico was a fine state, and the little girl turned her attention to us as Jackson and Foster talked about the buttes and scrub brush and the way storms seemed to roll right down the mountains and explode on the plains. The little girl shook at that.

Her whole body trembled. Sombra tried to comfort her, but the girl rolled out of her lap, under the table. Soon enough I felt her curled against my boots. I resisted the urge to reach down and touch her hair. Jackson and Foster changed the subject— back to money—and she calmed.

Almost forgot she was there. As I made to get up, I felt her weight against me. My movement woke her and sleepily she emerged from the table, covered here and there with crumbs and dirt. They didn't seem to bother her none. She lifted her hand and I took it in mine and together we walked back to my train car.

"Going to be here long?" she asked as she climbed under the blue blanket.

"Seven days at the most." Jackson had never stayed in a place longer than that. This town was a speck, a speck that didn't have a name anyone knew, and while the people might be hungry for what we could give, they wouldn't have much money. Santa Fe would be better, but Jackson had his mind set on heading farther west, toward the coast if possible.

She was restless in her sleep, kept kicking and shoving me. Finally, I moved away from her, sat in my chair and smoked a cigarette. It was cold, but the snow had stopped for the moment.

Where had she come from? What had she been doing out on that track? Most things we saw on the tracks were either there by mistake or looking to end their lives. Two years ago, Jackson obliged a young man by the name of Coleman Bean. After that, Jackson didn't stop his train for anyone. Till a few days ago.

She twisted and turned and finally sat up, her hair in a big clump on the left side.

"Could sleep better if the clouds would stop."

I crumpled my cigarette in the tin tray and stood. Above the mattress, there was a cargo door and I unlatched the squeaky hook and rolled it open. Above the mattress now, the sky was that soft pink that comes before a snow. The girl shivered, but not from the cold.

Making things disappear is easy if you think about it, but most folks don't think. I couldn't make the clouds disappear; I hadn't fully mastered clouds or water or flowers. But I could move them along, so I did. Willed them to move on toward Texas. The little girl stopped shivering once the pink sky turned black and the stars made themselves known. She relaxed back into the blankets and I got under with her.

"There's Jupiter," she whispered and extended a long arm beyond the covers. I swear she almost touched that planet with her pointer finger. She sure did blot it out for a moment or two.

"And Mars, but you know, I think I like Saturn the best."

Her little voice broke apart as she ended that sentence and she began to tremble again, like she'd done at the dinner table. I reached for her forehead, thinking to soothe her fear away, but she slapped my hand away, scooted to the other side of the mattress.

"Don't take it away," she said. "It's all I have left."

I did not question her, for it made sense to me. Fear could be a good friend. Lord knows fear had kept me alive during some pretty long nights. It was keeping me awake right now, wondering what the thing beside me was, for though it looked like a young girl, I knew it was not. It was something else, but I still had no name for it.

She slept then and I left the mattress, tossing the warmed blanket over her before I walked away. I went to my table and picked up the quarters and made them dance over my fingers before making them vanish entirely. They didn't slide up my sleeves and they didn't go through the cracks in the table.

Without the clouds, the air outside was bitter. I turned up the collar of my coat and buttoned it. The ground crunched under my feet and laughter carried to me in the frosty night.

The Doshenkos were practicing in the main tent, flying through the air with the greatest of intentions. They never seemed to get it quite right. Pasha slipped from Oleg's hands and plummeted to the netting where she somersaulted. Oleg laughed and so did Pasha. Perhaps one day, he said and she echoed it while climbing back up to try again.

Away from their circle of laughter it seemed colder, and I hurried my steps to the weird sisters' tent with purple and gold stripes. I kneeled before the flap and listened, listened so hard that I could hear them breathing inside. The air was spiced with incense here, sandalwood and lavender, and I took a deep breath.

It merged with their own and for a moment we breathed together. It felt as though I were inside the tent, snuggled between ample breast and small, and then as abruptly as I'd been there, I was here again, kneeling in dirt.

I didn't have to dig deep; the quarters were not buried far. All six of them were right where I'd sent them and this time none of them melted. They weren't a lost thing to me. Not this time. I gripped them hard, till their edges pressed into my fingers.

Things were easy to lose; hanging on to them took talent. Making things vanish was easy, if you knew where to send them. Knew the exact place as well as you know your own hands.

And I knew this place, this dark and spicy doorway, for many men had kneeled and gone through—this one included—but not tonight. I took my quarters and whispered goodbye to the sisters before taking my leave.

The little girl was sitting in the doorway to my car when I returned. Her thin legs swung restlessly. She wanted to run, but didn't know where to go. Wanted to vanish, but didn't know where to put herself.

"We go west from here?" she asked. Her hands plucked at her shift. "I heard the man, Jackson, say west. We can't go west."

I pocketed my quarters and looked at her, wondering exactly how she meant to stop this train and its people from going west. I waited for an answer and she only grew more agitated. The shift was shredding under her fingers; she was plucking hard enough to tear the thin fabric.

"I can't go west." And she was firm about that. "Not even if there's more hot rolls and marmalade. East," she said, finally giving me a clue. "And a little south. Would that be so hard? Won't Jackson reconsider?"

"There's nothing that way. Jackson goes where the people are, where the money is. Has his mind fixed on San Francisco eventually. I think he's got family there." Did she notice the way my voice caught on that word, family? Her sharp eyes didn't miss much; they were narrow now, as though she meant to study me the way I'd been studying her. *Don't do that, little girl,* I thought and she sat straighter.

"East."

She turned her face up to the stars, but Saturn didn't lay in the east so I didn't figure it was a star she was following. "What's east?" I asked and she didn't look at me. Didn't turn away from the stars. Didn't even answer me.

And before long, it was too cold to just stand there, so I had to go inside. I started a fire in the small grate, warmed my hands and my feet, and made sure the smoke wouldn't roll back on us during the night.

It didn't roll back on us, just on me, for when I woke she was still out there looking at the stars. I saw her point to one and heard her say, "I am there."

But she wasn't there—she was here—and that was her entire problem.

———

She hadn't meant to come to Earth, she told me. It was all one big mistake. She'd been running from her family, had to get away, and this is where she ended up. She had to stop running because her ship stopped. Caught something in the engine and when she was about to get it right, a New Mexican storm slapped her down. Two years, that's how long she'd been here, trying to figure a way back home.

Two years ago, Jackson had stopped the train for a young man named Coleman Bean. A lot could happen in two years.

Couldn't find any of her own kind. Seemed she was the only one, and that thought filled her with an agony that tasted like metal in the back of her throat. She'd climbed onto the tracks to kill herself, but damn Jackson had to go and stop. Had to find that shred of soul within himself and put it to use that night.

"You was glowing like some firefly," I said. "I think that

might have caught his attention. Maybe he thought you was a diamond." I grinned and she shoved me. She didn't look like a diamond or a firefly.

I didn't mean to come to this place, either, I finally told her, though it wasn't Earth I was meaning. This circus train. But I'd been running, too, and yes, away from family. Sombra and Gemma spotted me in a track-side bar, performing card and coin tricks for a little cash. They told me they had a better deal, both in and out of their tent. They were right, so I came to the tracks and watched the train slow as they said it would. Anything was better than going back.

"Going back is the only thing," she countered as she stuck her bare feet toward the flames. "Until you do, you're in limbo. Fancy Earth word. Why'd you run?"

"Why did you?"

She didn't answer me and I didn't answer her, and the night blurred into morning as we warmed our feet beside the darkened grate.

The first night of the show is perhaps the best. Mistakes happen, but that's part of the fun. Like Manny and his lions; surely he didn't mean for the male to eat his red coat, but it happened. Buttons and all, down the hatch, and the audience applauded while the big cat licked his lips.

We didn't have many animals in the show. The monkeys seemed to be the favorites, but Miss Victoria Solace didn't appreciate the way they stole her hat and wore it around the ring. They pranced and chattered and the men roared and pointed. I made the hat vanish from the monkey's paws and reappear on her head, much to her delight.

Mrs. Isabel Tompkins had the kind of mind I liked, clear

and warm like a summer pond. I could see everything that lay under the surface and when she handed me her handkerchief and bade me "vanish it!" it was easy enough to do so. In her mind I could see her orderly kitchen, though her husband Harry was always fussing with the bread box and tinkering under the sink and she wished he would stop.

I couldn't make him stop, but I took her handkerchief and folded it in half. In half again, and once more. I folded until I couldn't fold anymore, until the fabric had no more to give. And then I pinched the fabric between my fingers and it vanished. Isabel's eyes flew wide and the entire audience applauded and roared.

She expected me to pull the fabric from my sleeve. They always do. But I could only lift my hands and tumble away toward the next thing to vanish. She would find her handkerchief, folded between the kitchen table leg and the golden but scarred wood flooring. The table would have stopped its rocking, but it wouldn't occur to her to look for two months.

The little girl watched the entire show through the legs of an enormously fat man. She was pressed under the bleachers, and though she could have had a much better seat, she didn't seem to want one. I could understand the need to hide; coming to Jackson's had been a way of hiding. Couldn't live with Sherri Lynn anymore. Just couldn't.

Her mind was like Mrs. Tompkins, so clear I could see every thought and know them as if they were my own. I could see Sherri Lynn's past, could know how she felt about her daddy, and how she wished he would vanish. And it was all too easy after knowing that darkness.

All too easy to pluck him from the hardware store where he worked and bury him in the worm-rich mud beneath the shed of a house he had lived in twenty years before. Sherri Lynn hated that shed, but knew every corner of it. I took that memory, made it my own, and sent him there. The disappearance of Ralph Moody was never explained, though no one seemed to mourn him.

Still, it was that kind of thing that bothered me. I pictured that man, slowly suffocating in that dirt, and just couldn't live with the fact that I'd done it. Didn't matter that he'd touched Sherri Lynn wrong. Didn't matter that he hit his wife and called her names you wouldn't call a dog.

I couldn't pull him back out of the ground; once he was gone, he was gone. I tried, but couldn't budge him. Once a thing vanished, it was gone to me. Someone else could come upon him. He could be a found thing then, but to me he was a lost thing. Vanished. Except the quarters, I reminded myself. I was getting better. Maybe in time, things wouldn't have to be so lost.

"Rabi," the little girl said after the show. She slipped her long fingers into mine and handed me a stone. She had picked it from beneath the bleachers; I could feel the very depression it had made in the ground. Shallow and as cool as the night air.

In her mind, she showed me where she wanted the rock to go. The desert plain was lit by only starlight; the brush and cactus made strange shadows over the ground. In the ground, buried beneath rock and mud, was a piece of a lost thing. Metallic and not something I could fully understand. I tried to, but I felt the same murk I did when I tried to look into the little girl. She was giving me this, allowing me to see, but I couldn't understand.

The rock vanished from my palm and the breath went out of her. It was like wind moving through trees, that soft whooshing sound the leaves make. She made this sound, her hand relaxed in mine, and we continued on toward my train car, without another word spoken between us.

Come morning, Jackson was more excited than I'd seen him

in days. He interrupted everyone's practice and called us all to the main tent. Pasha Doshenko stayed on her trapeze, swaying above us as Jackson talked.

"It's a good deal," he kept saying while he rubbed his hands together and paced before the crowd of us. It's like he was trying to convince us, but he never had before. He'd always told us where we were going and those who wanted to follow did. A few had been lost along the way, but what better show was there than Jackson and his unreal circus and marmalade?

"There's a man, you see," he said, and I did see, a round man with round glasses and thick hands, and this man offered Jackson more money than he'd ever been offered for a performance. "Food and real shelters included," Jackson continued, and I saw in his mind a hotel with a swimming pool and everything. I saw warm baths and soft beds. "We'd stay for the winter, till things get warm again."

That part of the deal was important, I realized, and I felt the pain in Jackson's hands as though it was my own. He was young, but his bones had already started to rub together, causing him pain no matter how he moved. Jackson wanted to bed down somewhere warm for a few weeks and move on when spring came.

"Dallas," he finally said. Which was backwards from where we were going. It would delay San Francisco, he said and I got a flash of a woman in his mind. Not his lover, but perhaps his mother as he remembered her from his childhood. Jackson wanted to get home, wanted it badly, but didn't know if he could stand the winter ride to get there.

This was agreeable for the little girl who began to purr against my side. I'd forgotten she was there, but traveling east was fine with her and when Jackson took his vote, her long pale arm was one of the first to rise.

Didn't matter to me where we went, really, but Dallas was

a little too close for my comfort. Close to Sherri Lynn, close to the little house that had been ours. She was still there; she wouldn't leave her roses nor her turtles for anything in the world. She liked her teaching, liked being far from her family.

"Limbo," the little girl whispered and I wondered then if my mind were clear to her like Sherri Lynn's had been to me. "Goin' east, goin' east." She couldn't contain her excitement.

"What is it you want me to make vanish?" I asked, wanting this over. Once I did the trick, she would go. Wouldn't she?

But she shook her head and her pale hair rubbed her shoulders and then my coat as she nuzzled up to me. I went stiff under her touch. I didn't need this, didn't need her telling me I was in limbo. I wasn't. I'd moved on with my life, did what was best for me and Sherri Lynn both.

The little girl didn't answer, and I found out later that night that Gemma, now as dark as Sombra, and Sombra, now as light as Gemma, had named her Vara. Vara curled herself up at my grate once more and slept through the show, while I danced and performed until exhaustion claimed me and I made a man's vanished coin appear in a woman's all-too visible cleavage. He chuckled, she shrieked, but the play went on.

The train moved at a steady pace through the New Mexico desert. It was strange to see snow across cactus and scrub brush, over the red and taupe earth, but there it was and it looked pretty.

Vara didn't move from the small window much. She stayed huddled in the blanket and her breath made small puffs of fog on the pane. Every now and then she pressed her fingers against the glass, as if trying to measure distance. Once, she got excited about a landmark, but we passed it and she realized it wasn't the mountain she'd been thinking about.

She started wailing the next day, as the train drew closer to the state line. She woke me with her crying and there was nothing I could do to calm her. Her cries rose until the window shattered and the train ground to a sudden halt. Froze up on the tracks, as though it was caught in ice. Vara wrenched herself from my arms, scrambled out of the car, and across the frozen desert.

I watched her go, the tail of her shift flipping up and down like an antelope tail. She'd refused all offer of other clothing; didn't want anything that made her look human, she told Gemma. There was no danger of that, I thought, but kept my opinion to myself. She was too small and too pale to be human, but running away ... she had that down pat.

With the train stuck on the tracks, we weren't going anywhere for a while. Jackson's hot cursing should have melted the frozen wheels, but they remained wedged against the track, unmoving.

Gemma, back to her stardust self, shoved me and I stumbled into the brush. "Go after her," she demanded, and Gemma never demanded. Those hands coaxed and that voice tempted, but now they demanded and I went, following the trail Vara had left in the snow.

It was a wide trail, clumsy and crooked. Her feet must be frozen, I thought, but told myself they weren't human feet at all and maybe she didn't even feel the cold. The cloudy sky above me began to darken, though it couldn't be much past mid-day. My own feet were cold, legs stiff, and I didn't want to go much further.

Vara was sprawled on the ground ahead of me, one hand stretching toward the eastern horizon. I touched my hand to her back and found her like a block of ice. No matter that she wasn't human, she was cold and I picked her up and cuddled her into my coat. She was passive against me, maybe too cold to react, but when I turned away and headed back toward the train, she whimpered.

In my mind I saw a picture of what "east" meant to her, and I fell to my knees. They cracked against stone, but I couldn't feel any pain as I went down. Could only see and feel what Vara showed me then and there.

The metal was curved, the smooth edge of a ship meant for the stars. Her ship once upon a time, but now it was broken, most of it carried away. She couldn't get home, couldn't find her people, but wanted to get back to that one remaining piece of ship. And if she couldn't get there, she wanted to disappear.

It would be easy, I found myself thinking. Easy to make her vanish, into that bit of ground, nestled against the metal of her ship. But no, no, God, I just wouldn't do it. She was living and breathing and I wouldn't end that.

She felt my refusal, but was too cold and weak to move away from me. She pushed against my chest, made me feel all that she was missing—the touch of her mother's hand, the nuzzle of her lover, the familiar dirt of her homeworld—but still I refused.

Vara reached up and grabbed a handful of my hair. She yanked, tried to make me feel pain, any pain that would equal her own, but she couldn't and that only made hers more keen. She touched me again, this time deeper, and unlocked my own pain. Made me touch Sherri Lynn and the desolation she had known after I vanished. I had closed that off long ago, but Vara opened it as easy as she might a door.

Left that morning and didn't tell Sherri Lynn, couldn't tell her, and she woke alone in the bed. My things were neat in the closets and drawers, but I was gone. Gone like the fairies came and took me in the night.

Sherri Lynn was broken, like Vara's ship. Submerged in cold ground, buried so no one could find her. She was dying there, cold and alone, and here I was, playing in the circus without a care in the world. Accepting Beth's warm smile, finding comfort in Gemma and Sombra's bed. Taking time with ladies like Anne who came to visit and wanted something to vanish in exchange for a little roll and tumble. Pretending Sherri Lynn didn't exist.

It was easier than going back, but going back we were and if I wouldn't press Vara into her ground, she would press me into mine.

When Vara was ready to go, she released the train from its slumber. The wheels slowly turned and steam rolled back over the cars. Merrily we roll along, Jackson whispered and refused to look at Vara.

"Shouldn't have ever stopped for her," he said.

"She'd be dead then."

"Blown to bits like that cow," Jackson agreed and I knew he meant it.

The cow had been a spectacular thing, standing there one minute, flying in a thousand pieces the next. The train only slowed briefly. I could have moved it before we hit. But I hadn't. Why? Sometimes the simplest answers are the truth. I didn't want to. I wanted to see what happened. That was why any of us did anything. Just wanted to see what happened.

Making the cow disappear was easy, moving it just off the tracks to the lazy stretch of grass beyond. It would chew grass for a few more years, but it was stupid and would wander onto the tracks again sooner or later.

To Jackson, Vara was a stupid thing. A thing that would wander onto another track sooner or later.

She didn't move when I lay her down on the mattress. Her knees were still drawn to her chest. I covered her with the blanket and watched her, and wondered if I was wrong.

"You could find a life here," I finally said. "It could be a good one."

She roused at that. Sat up and turned toward me, stretching toes toward the fire I'd made. Vara shook her head. "I don't want to be something unreal, something people pay money to see. I just want to go home. And can't."

She picked up the thing nearest her hand, a discarded shoe, and threw it at me. I was so startled I didn't react and the shoe hit me in my chest. It fell to the floor as she yelled at me.

"And you can. Your home is there and you don't go."

"My home is here."

"This is no home." She pounded the mattress and gestured around her. There was little here that would make this a home; the room itself never existed in one place for more than a few nights. There was no yard, no flowers, no real bed with sheets and pillows. No photographs on the wall and no mail in a mailbox. No Sherri Lynn.

"I had to come here," I said as I reached for the shoe Vara had thrown. I picked it up, held it in my hands, used it as a focal point. Anything so I wouldn't have to look into Vara's eyes. "I did it to a man once, made him vanish, and it's too easy to do it again. I can't do it again, I won't. Not even for the best of reasons, don't you see?"

I think she did see, because she turned away from me. I dropped the shoe and crouched behind her, wrapped my arms around her small shoulders, and pressed a hand over her heart. Or whatever it was that fluttered inside of her like a caught fish.

"Right here and now you are alive. It don't matter that

you're different. It don't matter where you came from. No one is goin' to care about those things."

"But I care." Her voice was small, so small I could have held it in my palm and had room for a bird, a shoe, and maybe a jar of marmalade. "I am those things. And you, you have this wonderful gift and all you do is make coins roll down women's dresses. You could help me—I've shown you the place."

There would be no arguing. I'd known that all along.

"Then let's go, you and me. Let's go now." She turned in my arms and her eyes brightened. Her watery fingers squeezed my arms. She was ready now. She had nothing to pack.

And neither did I really, so when the train stopped for the night, we stole into the car of horses and took One Eye, who Jackson was always threatening to shoot. Grabbed some rolls and marmalade, and vanished into the night.

We weren't alone right away; Sombra and Gemma followed us, in shadows and bits of starlight, but they didn't talk so we didn't acknowledge them.

We rode that whole long night through and through the next day. We stopped only long enough to eat. Vara was too excited about getting to the place she'd shown me in her mind. Her mind was more clear now, she was showing me more things. Things I didn't really want to see, but couldn't help but noticing.

She had one thing on her world that she missed as much as she missed familiar faces. Smashed berries was all she could think to call it in her head. Like the marmalade, I thought as her pale finger slid into the jar to scrape the final sweet bits from the bottom.

Next twilight brought us to the place Vara had shown me in her mind. It wasn't a pretty place, barren and deeply scarred. Vara slipped out of my loose hold and ran across the snowy ground, light as a fleck of lint. She went over a small ridge and I rode One Eye down after her.

Vara kneeled in the dirt, took up handfuls of it and scrubbed it over her skin. This was the place, she'd lived here for a month before she'd found the courage to leave and look for her own kind. But there were none, only tall, dark strangers who didn't speak her language and so she had to learn.

"I want to go, will you make me vanish?"

I got off One Eye, slow because I could feel the ground vibrating with her excitement. Came to her side and kneeled down there, touching the dirt that covered her and then the ground itself.

That metallic thing was under there, the piece of her ship, and I could feel the small remains of another of her kind. Not much left, maybe a finger or toe. Whatever else had been taken away with shovels. I could still feel the deep grooves they'd made that day in the dirt.

"Rabi."

Her dirty fingers curled into my shirt sleeve and I shook my head. "Can't put you in this ground," I whispered. "You'll die. Do you have death on your world?"

Of course she did, it was a stupid question. She knew exactly what she was asking here. There was no hesitation in her eyes or her mind. Her hand tightened in my sleeve and she bent to her knees, as if they'd grown too watery to hold her.

"Not going home is already like death."

The truth in that hit me hard, so hard that I saw it then—a clean green orb hanging in the heavens. The cool of an alien wind brushed over my arms, made my hair stand at attention. An alien sun sank into a topaz sea, and all around me, birds that were not birds whirled and cried. I tried to breathe, but could not. Couldn't take breath until Vara stopped touching me.

I breathed, but the image of the place did not leave me. I

could see the flowers and the pollen on the flowers, and the small bugs embedded in the stems. I could see a structure, not like any house I knew, but it smelled friendly and tasted like love. I opened my mouth and took it whole, and as I swallowed, Vara's excitement rippled over me and tasted like smashed berries.

I focused on that small house and its taste. With Vara's small hand in mine, I could nearly feel the door, and it seemed to move under my fingers. Swinging inward, it revealed to me a room with a fire and a tall, tall figure, and I knew this was Vara's family. Felt it as though it was my own.

When I looked at Vara, her face was smooth, like someone had pulled a sheet of pale plastic from chin to forehead, sticking a finger in to leave a mouth hole. Vara's hand wasn't a hand, either; no hand like I knew. Under her vaguely human cloak, she was nothing I understood, nothing I could understand without a hundred lifetimes to do so.

But I could understand the things in my head. Family and warmth and water and bright skies lit by a shining star. I thought about those things, about those things through Vara. I thought about Vara, about her under that bright sky, pale toes in the golden water. I pictured her there and she giggled as though she already were.

She began to melt in my hands, pale sugar water running into the red dirt. Her mouth was still open in a dark O, her eyes wide with surprise—was it surprise or fear? Oh, it was fear. It stabbed me hard in the chest and I tried right then, tried so hard, to stop her from vanishing. Was it going wrong? I didn't know. Couldn't know.

"Vara," I whispered, but that had never been her name and her alien mind did not recognize it.

Once a thing goes, it goes. She was becoming a lost thing to me and no matter how I tried to hold her together, she still slipped through my fingers. She was going somewhere I could no longer find her, a place I could not even imagine without her guidance. She was cold and wet and then nothing at all. I felt an indistinct, lingering sense of her, a shimmer of warmth wrapped up in smashed berries. Then, nothing at all.

The cold began to seep through my trousers and I became aware of the light across the horizon. It had stopped snowing and the sun was coming up.

I guided One Eye out of the small depression and we kept moving east. Would have been easy to ride back to the train, but I couldn't go back, not now. Not going home is already like death.

Sherri Lynn was shoveling snow from her walk when I saw her two days later, her nose reddened from the cold, a green hat mashed over her pale hair. She looked up at the sound of horse hooves on the cold ground, stiffened when she saw it was me. I got down, but didn't come any nearer.

She extended her hand, slow and shaking, and I placed my own within it. Sherri Lynn's mind was now dark and cloudy. It was a blessed darkness and I loved the things I could not see.

"Coleman," she whispered, disbelieving.

That voice was familiar, warm with an uneven edge. I squeezed her hand and she whispered once more. I vanished into her voice, into the memories that flooded her, that flooded me. Familiar, haunting places that tasted like love and marmalade.

ARTIFICIAL NOCTURNE

1936, NEW ORLEANS, LOUSIANA

Rosemary and mint drip from the impossibly long fingers of Maman Floss as she spreads cooling bat grease across my shoulder. I keep my eyes closed, her voice wrapping around me in a contralto so soothing I forget the constant pain that radiates from shoulder to fingertips.

She tells me: *If I had broken you earlier, chauve-souris, you would not feel such agony. I should not have taken you, but sometimes you see a thing and cannot resist. You can see what it should be and make it such.* Her fingers slide down my arm, to the elbow where the bones have been separated. One bone is angled down, to support the silken, umber skin Maman Floss stretched into my wing. She holds me by the hand and stretches my wing until I whimper. Only then does she release me. In the right light—the gauzy light at the edge of the sodden marsh that spills above the steel train track—the edges of my wings flare with gold.

Maman Floss was broken before she can remember, changed from what she had been born as to what she would become. Her fingers were opened, spread, and lengthened when young muscles and bones still allowed such ease of puzzle-making. Her legs were unknotted, pulled like the taffies she sometimes brings home from the city.

Her great oblong head brushes the ceilings as she moves through her house and she bends through every doorway, honeyed curls catching at cobwebs. Her figure is perfect, retaining the shape of the hourglass that molded her throughout her youth. The fragments of that hourglass fill a jar that sits on the topmost shelf in the room I like least.

When the body is older, she has told me, it becomes more difficult, less flexible. *Flex-e-bull*, she says, voice thick with an accent from over the ocean. She wishes every day that she could spare me the pain as she does others in her collection, but she cannot, so we go forward as we are.

She tucks my winged arm against my side and I open my eyes, quivering after the rubdown. Gliding still exhausts me; my muscles are still developing to their form. Maman Floss twists the lid onto the jar of grease and wipes her pale fingers clean on her skirt as she crosses the room. She studies the casks and jars upon the shelves, the forms inside. Small hands press against the jar walls, palms traced with little lines that will never grow larger, grins warped by the ripple in the knee-high glass. Kage raps on his jar lid and Maman Floss goes to him, unscrews the lid, and lets him pop his head out. She talks to him in a soothing coo and then it's back into the jar he goes, content, still adapting his size to its glassy walls.

Of the dwarves, Gordon is my favorite. Maybe it is because I've known him the longest. Maybe it is because he holds my hands and dries my face when I am done crying. He doesn't tell me not to cry but lets me have a proper bawl, understanding the pain that comes from transformation. He's twenty-nine years old but smaller than even me. I can reach the counters in the kitchen; he has to climb up the stepstool to perch on them, which he has done now, bringing me a pineapple.

He sits beside me, parting the fruit with a knife well-suited to his smaller hands, offering me a gold crescent when it breaks free with a wet slurp. Sweetness bursts through the rosemary and mint, obliterating it.

Maman's father, Lucien Delaunay, requires the best things, even if it means making them himself. He often smells like paints and solvents from hours in his studio painting and creating. He paints our likenesses on broad sheets of crisp paper. Everyone in the house gives him a wide berth but for Maman Floss. He didn't have to assemble his car, but we treat it as though he did. When the car isn't being used, it rests under a cloth that reminds me of Maman's dresses, dark and soft between my fingers.

We don't do many things together as a family, so when Lucien says we are going to the city, there is a small explosion of excitement in every room of the house, even from those who aren't going. A trip into the city means we will return with unusual things: caramels, pomegranates, fresh coffee. Solomon, whose face has been remade into the likeness of a fish, wants a train; Harriet, who looks like she could fold her ears around her face to hide away, wishes for a yoyo. Maman Floss has Gordon make this list, as she cannot write so well with her long fingers.

Last winter, Maman Floss made me a new square-shouldered cape and she drops this over me as the list grows, helping me arrange arms and wings beneath the houndstooth fabric. Coconuts, ropes of garlic; Miriam wants a rocking horse but Lucien says no, absolutely no, because she is being made to tumble not ride, her legs and arms already loose, without joints. Gordon doesn't add it to the list, though he skips a space, as though it is there.

The grill of the car looks like long chrome teeth in a yawning mouth. Gordon said that once, but Lucien didn't like it, so Gordon has never said it again. Still, I can't stop thinking about it as the soft cloth is drawn back. The night-black of the fabric whispers away to reveal the metallic ruby curves and the thing I can never stop looking at, the small naked silver woman who perches at the apex of the hood. She is bent with the wind and a shiver runs through my whole body. I'm still looking at her when I crawl into the backseat. She is a bright speck through the windshield.

I call her Birdie and she sees us safely to the city, even though after a while I cannot see her for the way Maman Floss leans into her father and he wraps his arm around her narrow shoulders. I watch the way his fingers stroke the long line of her neck and the way she stretches in response, a cat about to purr. Her head brushes the ceiling of the cab, honey curls rioting, and I am reminded of the way her mouth moved against his skin in the room where she keeps the fragments of the hourglass that once enclosed her. I feel carsick and look at Gordon, who folds his list into triangles, back and forth, opened and closed, like a small blooming flower.

Marshland abruptly gives way to the city, building after building of wonder. Houses, markets, and workplaces spread out in precise rows. Some windows are hidden behind wood shutters whose faded paints have begun to peel from too many scorching summers. Other glass has been fashioned into long rows of thin doors that reflect twisted iron balconies clinging to stucco and brick alike. The two-story balconies with their iron arches are my favorites. Many are hung with gold-trimmed flags: scarlet, grape, the blue of Maman's Friday dress. These fluttering flags taught me my colors.

I don't go to the city often; my cape makes little sense in the summer and I cannot go in public without it. It hides my wings, which Maman says will alarm the common folk. They have never seen a wonder such as me, she says, and would hurt me in their excitement. Gordon is less troublesome, she also says; he is only small, often mistaken for a child. People look right past his ordinariness. But Maman Floss knows I love the city and so takes me in the cooler winter nights. It will be Mardi Gras soon, but already the city is illuminated.

We park at the end of the long market. When Lucien sees that I've nose-printed the window, that I have left a round of fog from my gaping mouth, he clicks his tongue. He snaps his hand as if he means to hit me but only pulls his handkerchief from his coat pocket, to wipe all trace of me from the glass. Gordon clasps the edge of my cape and we trail after Maman Floss, quickly forgetting Lucien. He will find us or not, but either way, we are already in the market bathing in the scents and sounds.

The market has its own language, a blend of Creole, English, Spanish, French. My first time here it was overwhelming, but now it's a comfort, a music that rises and floats into the night where I imagine lightning bugs suck it up and glow. The air coming off the river is cool tonight and it smells like mud, the kind I want to squish my toes into, but Gordon is already pulling me toward the heaps of produce. Maman Floss has a basket which we fill with coconuts (three), sausages (four links), and soft apricots (seven, but she gives me one now and I rub its soft hide against my cheek before biting into it). A group of nuns streams past us, black cloaks and white hats that seem to fly up onto the wind.

The earthy scent of mud gives way to fruit and vegetables the deeper into the market we go, but even above that, there is something else. It's not the boats that line the river docks but the long shadowed train on the tracks in front of them. It smells like a normal train, like oil and coal, but it smells like animals, too. Like lions to start, but then other things I've never smelled before. Things that smell like cloud and sky, and only when Maman Floss strokes her fingers down my nose do I realize that I've stopped walking and am staring.

She can smell these things, too, because her majestic head turns that way as if she's following my stare, but I can see the flare of her nose, the rise of her chest as she breathes in the air and knows something unusual has arrived. She continues down the row of vendors, ever closer to the train and its cargoes.

Crates of apples and long strings of bananas lead us toward smaller stands of instruments and books, toys and trinkets. Maman Floss finds a palm-sized train and a yoyo, and there is a rocking horse with a brilliant blue saddle but we leave her there, rocking under the force of a five-year-old who tackles it with glee. *Miriam's horse*, I think but do not say.

We creep toward the train, basket filling with items as we go. I can tell that Maman Floss is distracted when she buys more apricots, when she doesn't notice that I eat two more and pocket the stones, and I strain to see around her. I think at first that a long string of bananas is somehow sitting on top of the train, and how strange that is, and of course it would catch Maman's attention, but it's not bananas. People in the market shift, allowing the light to spill upward, and I easily recognize the line of a wing.

The great bird sits atop the train, its back to the market. It is impossible to tell the color of the wings in the play of light and dark, but they are beautiful, perfectly folded one over the other to mimic the shape of a heart against its back. I have never seen a bird so big; nor likely has Maman Floss, who stops in her tracks. Gordon, watching a line of monkeys being led past on a leash, runs into Maman, and I reach out to keep him from falling.

Scrolling text decorates the train's engine, gold curling into red and blue. *Jackson's Unreal Circus*, it says, with *Mobile Marmalade* scribbled below. I picture marmalade oozing from the train's wheels but see instead a small kiosk set up with row upon row of gleaming jars. They are stacked gems in the night, catching all available light, turning it to orange, gold, crimson.

Before I can ask if we can get some marmalade, Maman is moving that direction. It's rare that we are allowed this treat, too, but Gordon and I love marmalade spread on croissants, on baguettes, on anything. We would eat it off our fingers—and have.

The bird has eyes as golden as some of those marmalades. I belatedly realize this means the bird is watching me the way I watch it—the way I watch *her*. As I linger behind Maman Floss, hugging our full basket of purchases against my chest, my eyes are drawn upward to that large shadow which becomes less shadowy as she turns to watch us. It is with a soft cry I realize the bird has no bird's face.

She—*Oh*, her face is a human woman's, as if she has been made the way I have been made, a girl turned into a flying thing, but I can tell she has not been. There are no arms, no legs. From the neck down, she is bird and bird alone—but for that face. In this light, no longer blocked by the market stalls, her feathers glisten, seeming black but being red under that, blood trapped under ink.

Maman Floss reaches back, a comforting hand sliding over my shoulder and then away. She murmurs, but it's the marmalade lady she's speaking with, buying a jar of lemon and what I hope is cherry. These come into the basket, a solid weight, but I can't stop looking up at that bird. That beautiful bird.

Lucien finds us eventually and we leave the market as we came, Maman and Lucien exploring the shops she hasn't yet, me and Gordon trailing behind. I keep stopping to look at the train and its bird. And strangely, that bird is watching me, head tilted as though she is listening to a song only she can hear. Her immense talons curl against the metal of the train and I am captivated in a way I never have been before.

It's Gordon's small hand and whisper that gets me to look away. He pulls my cape hem, guiding me toward a column plastered with papers and posters. Lucien and Maman are haggling over the cost of grapefruits, so we are free to stare at the bulletins and to find amid them our own faces. Gordon's hand strokes the likeness of my face, my spread bat wings. I last saw this image in Lucien's studio, paint still gleaming wet. Now, there are words below.

Winter evenings, it says in a careful hand, *French Market.*

These posters are common in the market; people selling what they will, how they can. And I realize now that while Maman and Lucien might be talking about grapefruits, they look at me and Gordon and to the shop owner again, as though *we* are the tart round fruits in a bin, ready for inspection. But the shopkeeper says something Lucien doesn't care for and then we are gone, scooped into his arms, basket and all, carried up and out of the market, bundled back into his beautiful car, Birdie guiding us home.

Once home, I cannot stop thinking about two things: the bird and the poster. I am not sure which one disturbs me more. I don't tell anyone, not even Gordon. He doesn't speak to me of what we saw either, but there is still a conversation there, every time we look at each other. In his eyes, I see the same thing that must linger in mine. Questions and hurts. Have we been made only to be sold?

Of course we wondered what happened to the others who used to live in this house. People as curious as us, usually children but sometimes not, would come and go; Maman Floss said they came for her expertise, and after they got what they needed, they would return to whatever lives they had lived before. I could name them all, but I don't, because I wonder now if Miriam and Solomon will someday add my name to that list. The Curious Who Used to Live with Maman.

I could ask Maman, but I don't do that, either. She and Lucien are busy in the coming days and spend time in their room with the door closed. When once I would have sought Maman out for comfort, I now stay as far as I can; wandering the property, watching the trains as they speed past, toward the city and away.

While I wander the marsh and yard, through air that has a presence all its own, the plan begins to take shape in my head. The city is too far for me to reach on my own. I cannot walk there, nor glide all the way. My wings are not strong enough for flying and may never be, Maman Floss has told me; they are artificial, primarily for show, never meant to hold an entire body aloft no matter how skinny I stay. But I could reach the city on those trains, could glide my way to the top of a car and ride until I reached the market, the siren. There are things I want to know—things I know Maman will not tell me. If she would, surely she would have by now.

A bird like the siren? I think of those wings, and the skies, and all she must have seen. All the cities and people, the twisting rivers, some maybe larger than even the Mississippi, and the roads, and where those roads go. What does the world look like from those high places?

Gordon does not tell me no. Much the way he lets me cry, he doesn't argue when I tell him I mean to go. He does tell me to be careful, that if I want to go to Mardi Gras I won't be caught, and I very much want to enjoy the parades and spectacle, so I swear to be careful. *The trains run like clockwork*, he says. I can go and come back and no one will know, because also like clockwork are Maman and Lucien once that door is closed, once the lanterns are lit.

Catching the train is like catching lightning. It's fast and hot and stinks. From the roof of Maman's house, I ride an updraft of cool air and ride this west to the tracks but am unprepared for the speed of the train. I think it will be a simple thing to latch onto it—how the siren sat with her beautiful talons curled against her train!—but the train doesn't care that I am trying to land. It zips past as if I am no more than a speck of moss blown up from the track. I may as well be.

It's the last coal car I fall into, hard, and I lay there stunned, watching the starry sky unfurl as we move away from the house. By the time we reach the city, I've gathered myself enough to realize I have no cape, no protection from common eyes. Before the train can completely slow, I lift my arms to catch the wind, to let it carry me out of the coal and toward flat rooftops.

The wind has its own language. I do not yet know all of the words, but I know enough of them until I reach the edge of the last building. There is an unexpected updraft, the rush of a competing wind from the street, and it buoys me up before dropping me. I tumble into the cobbled street near the empty marmalade stand.

For a little while, it's quiet. The market is closed and the rumble of that far off train stays far off. If I listen close, there is the sound of the river, but that's not what I came for. The circus train is still there. I push myself up from the ground, arms held close to my sides to hide my wings as I run to the tracks.

West of the market and running parallel to the river, there is a triangular open space. Circus tents fill this space, striped and not, luminous in the dark. Shadowed figures move inside some while others are still. I can smell wild cats the closer I get and see that they are not caged but prowl the fence that encloses the entire circus. A lioness spies me, a regal head I know only from the one that decorates the wall in Lucien's studio. The eyes that appraise me are not glass. They hold a hunger I don't want to see. Even with the fence there, I run.

She bolts alongside me. The fence line blurs between us, my arms and legs pumping. But I am a poor runner, my wings slowing me, and if this fence did not stand between my strides and hers, the lioness would be upon me. Her snarl makes me shriek and then I am airborne. The ground falls away and I seem to be flying but I am not. Hard talons curl over my shoulders, around my arms, mindful of my wings. I look up to see who I came for: the siren.

She carries me over the fence line inside the circus limits and sets me down near a metal barrel that is blazing with warmth and fire. The lioness keeps her distance, but I still stumble backward over a log, which has been dragged close to the barrel. I bite my tongue and splutter blood as the siren nears. She strides forward on those talons, takes hold of the log opposite me, and perches.

If beauty were a thing ... No. If the impossible was made possible ... No.

Just as the wind has its own language, so too must whatever world this siren comes from. I cannot find the words for her.

She watches me with her golden eyes, and I think that she must be draped in jewels to gleam the way she does but it is only feathers and firelight. I pick myself up and slide onto the log, wrapping my awkward wings around my shaking body. The siren does not waste time with hellos.

"You are trying to be a bat," she says.

That isn't entirely correct and I open my mouth, but the siren lifts a wing before I can speak.

"You have been made into a bat," she says next, "but were a little girl before this? Are still a little girl ... but one with bat's wings. Who has done this thing to you?"

"Maman *saved* me."

The tone in my voice startles me. Startles the siren, too, because her shoulders lift, her head tilts, as if absorbing a blow. But then she smiles, and I am somehow telling her the story, the story of a girl so tiny she could fit through a whisper space between brick buildings if she had to (and she had to), a girl so tiny she could walk through puddles without leaving a ripple. A girl who did not know her parents but had been given up to the city, because the city seemed a kinder mother than one who spent all her money on tobacco and alcohol. This was a girl who was found by Maman Floss shivering in the rain until a velveteen coat was wrapped around her, until she was drawn into a beautiful car and carried away, to a house in the marsh filled with children like her, children who would be remade into things as beautiful as that car.

"You are Gabrielle," the siren tells me, and from her talon she tosses a scrap of paper, the poster with my face and name. "I am Agnessa."

Agnessa tells me her own story, about how she lived with others of her kind until one day hunters came, hunters with arrows which sliced the sky apart and sent her sisters to death. She alone survived the slaughter and lived because of the kindness of one man and one woman, these two emerging from a place she can still hardly believe, and at that she gestures to the circus which enfolds us. We are similar creatures, she tells me, having survived the worst things, but the difference is this: she has freedom, I have captivity.

There is a denial in my mouth—it tastes metallic—but I know she is right. I had to sneak away to be here. I could not tell Maman I was coming, but even so, she knows, because Agnessa turns as we hear the crunch of tires over gravel, as that crimson car pulls up outside the line of the circus fence and Maman steps out to regard us.

Maman never yells. She takes me home, pressing fairy-soft apricots into my hands for the ride back. At the house, I worry the storm will come from Lucien but I don't see him. Maman leads me into the kitchen, sits me on the stool beside the counter, and cleans my face. I am a mess of apricots and coal dust.

Chauve-souris, she whispers. *What if someone had seen you? What if someone had taken you from me?* And when I don't answer, she keeps on, her hands as tender as ever as they slide through my wet hair. I can feel each coil spring back as she passes through. *I could not bear such a thing ever, ever.*

She encourages me to go back, insisting that Gordon accompany me. *It will be difficult,* she says, *because Gordon cannot fly, but go, speak with the siren, learn her ways, test your wings.* That same rosemary mint smell falls from her fingers as she strokes a shiver down my arm.

I never dreamed of being allowed to go this way, and though the going is slower with Gordon, we find a farmer who makes the trek every day and doesn't mind a couple curious occasional passengers.

For tales of our lives, he will take us. He thinks every word is a fiction. When I tell him of Maman's grand head, of the way she lived her earliest years with it pressed between cloth-wrapped boards, he laughs, for the image of this young girl is a strange one. How did she see to walk, the farmer demands. She had no need, I say, because of what had been done to her legs, her arms. She could not walk as she was being remade.

I, too, am being remade. Agnessa welcomes us with open wings. Every time thereafter, it is also a welcome. Gordon and I sit amid the performers as they practice. The gates are closed during the day to allow preparation for the evening shows. They will have a float in the parades, Agnessa tells us. They will shower the crowds with beads, coins, and if someone is very lucky, free tickets to all the circus shows.

The marmalades are sweet and tart both, and while they don't evoke a response in me other than hunger, Gordon is drawn to tears with every bite. It reminds him of Paris, he says as he folds a bit of croissant together with orange marmalade and tears pressed between, and I never knew he was in Paris— don't even know where that is, but I picture deserts and flowing sand. He says no more, swallowing the bread, tears and all. Beth who makes the marmalades only smiles like she knows. Jackson, who owns the circus, asks about Maman Floss and Lucien. He has seen the posters, he prompts. This reminds me I am to be sold.

Jackson never asks about that. He only smiles like Beth as Agnessa leads me to the main tent and shows me the trapezes. They hang in pairs from the tent ceiling and we watch as the humans swing upon them, and leap, and soar. My heart aches for it and when Agnessa nudges me toward the long rope ladders that lead up, I stumble. I could not—

Mother birds don't push their young from the nest, Agnessa tells me as she walks me over. But her mother was not precisely a bird and so felt no such need to hold back and shoved her out with one strong wing. Agnessa screamed the whole way down but before she could hit the ground unfurled her wings and flew. Flew away and never looked back, until she was captured.

The ropes sag under my weight, but soon I am at the top and no one there looks at me like I am out of place. They step back and give me the platform, one man holding a trapeze should I decide I want one. But I don't. I look down at Agnessa and don't think about anything as I let go and fall.

The air catches me, or I catch the air, and I lift myself up with one stroke and then another. But my body is too heavy for my wings, so I let the air guide me down in slow spirals, until I touch my feet to the dusty ground.

Agnessa beams. If beauty was a thing … No. If the impossible was made possible … No. There are just no words for that, nor when she has us climb upon her broad back and nestle between her wings. She smells like all the high places, where only wind and cloud go, and that's where she takes us, up and toward Maman's marsh house, where she leaves us, traces a wide circle in the sky, and is then gone.

<hr>

Fat Tuesday. Tonight, the nuns stay inside to prepare for the coming of Lent, and even the moon has tucked herself away this year. I cannot see the stars for the amount of light that vomits up from the bedecked streets. So many lights and candles and it doesn't matter that most people have no money; what little they had was converted to light, just for tonight.

Amid the floats roams the circus and its people. Not creations. They have not been made the way Gordon and I have been and I think my eyes should run green with envy. Each is a natural thing:

Agnessa the siren, Delilah the bearded lady, Prancer the man who is somehow as tall as rooftops; Foster who smells like the hot metal of fresh coins, and Sombra, who is a shadow against her sister Gemma until she turns into the light and Gemma the shadow. The lions prowl on leashes of cobweb and mist, and I can hardly stand the wonder. Gordon and I watch from the rooftops, trailing the procession. Maman Floss says she will meet us at the end, with hot cocoa because the night is cooler than any yet.

But she meets us with more than that. I don't notice until I'm on the ground, because the glide down is what I look forward to. Tonight of all nights, I can be me, because they will mistake me for a thing from the parade, possibly a wonder from the circus, so I need no cloak even though the air is cold. Gordon and I reach the last building and there is a rush of air and I unfurl my wings, to catch this and ride it down. I scoop this invisible air into the skin that Maman so lovingly stretched over my broken arms, the ordinary skin she made into extraordinary wings, and even when my feet touch down, I keep my wings spread. They ruffle like silk.

Gordon takes the fire escape to the ground and he's clapping for me, clapping and laughing until he sees Maman and the strange man at her side. This man is gaunt, his cheeks hollowed as though someone sucked him empty with a straw. But his coat is the color of Lucien's car and this draws me forward when perhaps I should show more caution.

Chauve-souris, Maman whispers and she draws me close, a hand under my chin. Her long fingers curl up along the side of my face to lift my gaze to that of the strange man. He looks at me without so much as a smile. He is intent, studious, and smells like dark leaves that have been dried in hot sun. When he takes hold of my hand to draw my wing back out, I pull back, but he doesn't let me go, and that's when I know. His eyes narrow and his hand hurts so badly around mine and he pulls me toward him. No.

My time spent with Agnessa and the flyers has served me well. For a moment that lasts too long, I give in to his pull. My feet whisper across the ground, and when he has me closer he eases his touch because he thinks ah, she has understood and given up as the smaller animal will give in to the larger. No.

This close in I tuck my wings and dive for the ground. He does not expect this, so I am gone as he turns, as Maman cries out.

These cries are lost in the sounds of the parade. I run blindly from the man she would sell me to. I picture her mouth on Lucien and stop only once, to vomit every carnival treat I have eaten onto the street which still gleams with gold light. And then, running, flipping into the air when I feel an uprush. Putting more distance between me and everything I know until I stumble against a fabric wall, until I sink into straw and it swallows me and I can only think thank you, thank you, before I sob myself to sleep.

Jackson finds me. I wake to find he has pushed the straw back, enough to allow me to breathe without inhaling it. There's no panic when I sit up, when I pick straw from my skin. He offers me a wide cup and I drink as if I have roamed the deserts of Paris, and it's sweet lemonade, the best thing I have ever known. Jackson already seems to know my plight.

"Your bitch *maman* has my Agnessa," he says, and he brushes his hands together to remove flecks of straw. His fingers are bent as if his muscles seized up on him, as if he knows the pain in my own body from being changed. "You could stay here. Would never sell you."

He draws a poster from his shirt pocket and his face is a misery as he studies it. "She does this." It's not a question. I realize this is partly why they came, why Agnessa took me in. Jackson has known. "She takes children and she ..."

I can hear the pain in his voice when he can't continue. *Remakes us*, I tell him. *Breaks us as she was broken.* And I know now it's not normal, and it is like an awful waterfall through me, the truth rushing. All those children who left the house ... where had they gone? I could name them all—but I don't, because ... Because. That Jackson understands this betrayal is plain on his face. He nods, folds the poster back up, slides it back into his shirt pocket.

"Could stay here," he says again.

Maybe later, I tell myself because it's like a dream, that idea. But not yet, not while Maman has Agnessa.

Jackson drives me out to the marsh, where the house sits amid the moss-draped cypress, where the crickets' call is louder than nearly anything. I see Gordon in the yard but no one else. Jackson waits in the truck. Trusting me. Gordon hurries to my side, clutching at me, warning me how angry Maman is and Lucien, too, and they are looking for me, but they have also—

There is an awful sound from the house, a body screaming like it is being torn in two, and I run because I know the sound a thing makes when it breaks. I don't care about Maman and Lucien. I don't even care about me right then because there is this feeling inside like I will die if I stay here, if I am sold, if I am not sold. I have glimpsed awful things—and there is more awful to come, for I can smell the blood—but I have also seen the beauty and the light; I have seen that the train tracks leave this place.

Maman has Agnessa strung up in the room I hate, the walls bright with lanterns. Metal loops now descend from the ceiling, rise from the floor, and even emerge from the walls. Maman has tied Agnessa every which way, with rope that burns into her wings, her legs. I scream my fury at all of them, and Maman and Lucien stare—they have never seen me like this. I have never been like this. Maman tries to talk sense into me, but Lucien approaches with another loop of rope.

This is where things go bad. Agnessa struggles in her bonds, shedding feathers in her fear. The lanterns shake with her fury, light wavering as if in wind. Lucien strides forward and his hands smell like oil, like angry bird. The rope rasps against my cheeks as he drops it over my head, loops it around my throat. I picture Maman bent before him, her own throat held tight in his fist as her mouth moves against him. *Chavre-souris*, she told me long ago, *it is our way*. But not mine.

I only go slack enough to draw him in. He smiles—*mon petite*, he whispers and draws the rope into his fist. I slip forward, looping the rope around his wrists and pulling as I slide between his legs. With a tug, we both go down, and Maman screams. She can hardly stand it, but her nature is two-fold: the breaker, the healer. She staggers, clumsy in her panic, but I am not once loose of that rope.

It's deliberate when I sweep a wing into a lantern and send it crashing. Oil and flame lick up the wall, across the floor. The ropes which bind Agnessa catch. Maman shrieks and it's not Agnessa she reaches for, but me. I dance away, throwing shutters open so the air floods in, feeds the flames. I dash more lanterns to the floor. The room is engulfed and the heat is tremendous as Agnessa's ropes burn apart. She falls and her massive wings calm the fire a second before it surges back up.

Agnessa and I flee the room as the ceiling crumbles and the house is madness around us. Casks and jars explode from heat, sending dwarves sprawling on uncertain legs. Gordon helps them up, small hands clasping small hands that should not be small from now on, lined palms being allowed to finally grow outside glass walls.

This house is ever making things and now makes more Curious Who Used to Live with Maman. They emerge from their hiding places and we save all we can. As the fire consumes the house, the bed of Jackson's truck becomes an ark for the strange, the misplaced. Gordon huddles in my arms under the canopy of Agnessa's blood and ink wings, and we leave this place where we were broken and healed, returning to tents and train, and the promise of open skies.

Agnessa shows them to me. One by one, she teaches me the language of the winds.

WE, AS ONE, TRAILING EMBERS

1911, CONEY ISLAND, NEW YORK

We two live as one, but also as two when we are able. When night deepens and the park grounds grow quiet, we can let everything else fall away. When night deepens, we each close our eyes and pretend the same thing: we are a single being, we are alone in our body, we make every choice on our own, for our singular self. We pretend there is but one torso rising from this pelvis, only one head and only one heart. There is not another arm or wing to find our selves entangled in, nor another set of our eyes staring at us. In the darkness, there is only one.

With eyes closed, there is a singular heartbeat, a solitary pulse, and when we stretch, there is no we. We becomes a miraculous "I," and I drift in this place, alone but not lonely. I don't know what lonely is or could be; it is not a thing we—it is not a thing *I*—know. There is always another, but for here in the quiet dark. Still, I must be careful; if I stretch the wrong way or try to turn over, I am instantly drawn back into the "we" that I actually am. I never sleep on my side, on my belly.

If I wake first, I keep quiet. I listen to the soft breathing at my side and try to match it. Breath for breath, I can hide and pretend the *we* is still an *I*. Still a *me*. But soon enough this illusion is broken; there is a deeper breath, a waking breath, a breath that says, "I am back and we are *us* once more."

Hazel eyes look upon hazel eyes, and that mouth with its morning-dry lips curls in a smile of good morning. Sleep-warm arms and wings tangle together and we cannot help but burrow closer. Morning was once awful, returning from wherever sleep carried us, coming back to the knowledge of this body, this world. We spend these first moments entangled; it will be all right, no matter what, say these slow caresses. We bend mouths to chests, to foreheads, echoing kisses dropped elsewhere.

These soft touches lead to harder ones and we come together every time; we share everything from the navel down, there is no way to not share such intimacies. We still marvel at it, two minds sharing an identical physical sensation at the exact same instant; two minds momentarily obliterated by the most intense thing we have known. Until—

There is a man—Mister Hoyt—who would cut us apart.

Mister Hoyt has created the finest freaks within the walls of Dreamland, but we who travel with Jackson's Unreal Circus and Mobile Marmalade are new to him, made by means other than his hands. We have been on display in the carnival park the entire spring, a limited engagement before our circus train moves on again. Mister Hoyt comes once every week, to study us. He wears a suit of wool no matter the weather, one fine-fingered hand clasped above his heart. Of his other hand, there is no sign; this suit sleeve hangs empty. He watches us with glassy eyes that narrow with unfulfilled interest. He studies us because we are not a thing that has been made by any human hand.

We are displayed on an elevated turntable, in broad daylight. Long have visitors to the carnival claimed there is trickery involved, especially when we were displayed within a tent at night, but these assertions were put to quick death when Jackson moved us outside; even Mister Hoyt stopped saying we had been sewn together—he can not stop looking at us, longing for us. No one seems to mind the heat of the sun or the stench of tar and the buzz of saws against lengths of lumber from reno-vations deeper in the park; they brave most anything to look at us.

The turntable is three feet around, enough to hold us and whatever Jackson means to display us with. Once he assembled a collection of taxidermied two-faced cats at our feet, mounded so high they constantly spilled over the edge; once it was a school of Fiji mermaids dangling on silver wires. They moved as we moved, nauseating in effect. Usually, as now, it is the frame of a cheval glass, within which we stand. Beneath the table, well-muscled dwarfs walk in countless circles to turn us about.

Smoke and mirrors is what they said early on, encouraged by Mister Hoyt, so that others would come see Hoyt's creations rather than Jackson's. Now, Jackson plays up the notion of mirrors, because at first glance, one cannot help but think we are a reflection. Today, flawless Beauty's reflection is that of Beast, while withered Beast gazes upon Beauty with an endless hunger. Only we and Jackson know the truth of it: we are each

Beauty and we are each Beast. Only by taking turns can we find the space to breathe and live.

They watch, captivated. Park visitors pay their coin and gather around our turning base, and watch as we rotate through the afternoon. It is summer now and the unbroken sunshine turns our wings to silver and gold. If you know where to look, you can see where we are shaded blue with quiet blood and sometimes the orange of a rousing blush. These hues are secret to most; had by others for another coin.

In the sunshine, only silver and gold, only Beauty and Beast. (Jackson once twined us inside rose vines sharp with thorns; there was a single rose, dark as heart's blood, held in the cleft of our waist, this for visitors to discover as we turned and turned.) We lift our hands—two without flaw, two withering down to bone—to the heat of the sun, allowing beaded sweat to run down our adjoined torsos. Within that hollow, sweat collects, then rivers down shared belly, shared legs. Some ladies cannot bear the sight—it is reflection only, one man reassures his wife as she turns her face away; she peeks from the safety of his shoulder, but she sees. In her eyes, we see that she understands.

She knows that this is one body, imperfectly and improperly made. She cannot tell if we are male or female, cannot know the flesh that lurks beneath the strip of silk that wraps our waist. She cannot judge by the fall of straight ginger hair, or the four hazel eyes which evenly regard her in return. But she can believe that in the making of us someone made a terrible error. We should have come from the womb separate, yet did not. Our mother, merely flesh and bone they say, was cut open so that we might live. But we think we came from the heavens. We remember a space without space, a world without end. Amen.

Later, this woman comes to our tent, this lady who could not look at us under the clear daylight. In the tent, the air is warm and occluded by the haze of cigars, cigarettes. Men have come, looked, gone, but the lady, she lingers, and without her husband she eyes us with more interest. We bow our heads and say nothing. Here, we cannot yet speak.

Jackson who owns the circus is quick to slither up to her, to stroke a rough hand over the fall of our ginger hair and tell the lady she can have us. Anything here might be had, enjoyed, consumed. We watch her with a kind of hunger, saliva on a tongue, ready to dissolve that pink mouth should it come near enough. Jackson makes his deal, a whisper of paper money between palms, and we guide the lady deeper into the tent. The things we do are not for others' eyes.

Here, the air feels cooler, the striped canvas covered in the fragmented shade of a tree outside. Here, we lead the lady into a room, where she sits upon a chair of padded velvet; she's surprised at this chair, this small piece of civilization amid the freaks. Nervous laughter accompanies this word; she doesn't apologize. She smooths her sweaty hands over her dress, over thighs and silken stockings. We watch these hands and her face in the same instant; she radiates want and curiosity, no longer the shame and fear she displayed outside.

We come to stand before her, nudging her knees open with ours. This bold approach surprises her; she sits straighter, drawing her spine in, her breasts out. Where her stockings end, we see the marks upon her, the scars of cigarettes pressed into skin. When we study these, there comes a sharp intake of breath from her. She paid for us, but her touch is slow to come, tentative. She touches a wrinkled arm and our eyes close. The world reduces to a pinprick; in the dark, I am singular, solitary. There is only she and me, the stutter of her damp fingers down my bare arm and then across our belly. This shared sensation is agony, pleasure and pain both because it is not wholly mine, yet within this communal knowledge there is a doubling of want, of need.

"Which of you is Idalmis?" she asks. Her breath is a warm flutter above the silk that still wraps our waist.

"We are," we say together, two separate voices that are of a melody together; contralto and baritone.

The woman doesn't know what to do with this information; that while we have two torsos, we have but one name between us. She looks from one to the other, and it's not confusion that crosses her features but determination.

Always give them what they pay for, Jackson has told us. They pay for our time, our attention, for the feel of four hands upon flesh. She has touched us, so now we touch her, fingers withered and not plucking at her cotton dress the way she plucks at the silk which hides our secrets away. And then, this silk comes away, and she sees how we are made, and she slides from that civilized velvet chair and takes our soft flesh into her pink mouth, and the world washes away.

We both feel that mouth and ride it to its inevitable end. Dead end, cul-de-sac, the place where all curls into a tight ball before it springs loose once more. And then, we've our hands in her hair; four hands and her eyes slit shut and she's riding her own wave, toward another dead end, an end she never sees coming. Beauty, wanting to be kind but unable, slides fingers into the woman's gaping mouth and pulls against teeth. Beast can only watch as the body comes apart—withered hands are not strong enough for this violence, withered hands cannot satiate this hunger. Fragmenting flesh blooms like flowers and is eaten petal by petal. Beast eats alone, but Beauty knows the pleasure of this moment even if Beauty cannot partake. Later, Beauty will drink cold white milk and steal bananas from the monkeys; Beauty will peel three bananas and lay them upon our thigh, eating each with five precise bites.

When all is done and the woman's skin is but a husk we toss into a back room, we clean each other in the shaded tent and step back outside to find Jackson with the lady's husband. He stands so tall in the afternoon sun, his shoulders broad. His hands look as soft as his wife's. Is he looking for her? Oh, no. He is looking for Idalmis, and after paper money whispers between palms we lead him into our tent. He smells like the cigarettes he once pressed into his wife's thighs.

Jackson knows our ways and never speaks of them—everyone hungers after all—not until he comes to our room and tells us the complication. The man was of the law, he tells us, and was looking for us, to question us about a body in New York. There will be others, when they realize he is gone.

There is no horror at this revelation—in Santa Fe, we consumed a priest, and there came others seeking to learn what had become of him. Jackson is not alarmed; there is a glint in his eye because he knows if there is trouble, Beast will swallow it away. Jackson's hands slide over our hair, the lines of our jaws, the bare expanse of our chests. We lean closer to him; he smells like the underbelly of a rotten house and we have no desire to eat him. But the praiseful stroking is pleasant and when he touches our wings with sure fingers, we shudder. He leaves us in our room, warned and ready for those who will come.

We know that in some places, people store food for times of famine. We have been unable to do this, travelling as the circus does on a train. Our time on this eastern coast will be limited—this carnival park is filled with freaks, and we are a special attraction. We are a limited-time offering; a thing glimpsed and then gone. We have no way to keep those who will come for later. Beast must suffer the gluttony.

At night, hundreds of clear lights illuminate the park, burning like miniature suns affixed to immobile poles. At night, we wander. Everyone stares, thinking this attention goes unseen under cover of darkness.

Mister Hoyt shadows us as we make our way; he carries with him a sweet scent that we know all too well, the scent of fresh meat, and we wonder who and what he has cut apart and created today. We look for him, expecting to find our selves reflected yet again in his glassy eyes, but he keeps well to the shadows tonight and we cannot pick his from among them.

Young boys trail more obviously in our wake, attempting to tread upon our wings which, when we want them to, trail upon the ground. Wing-tips flicker just out of foot's reach, frustrating the boys to no end. They leap closer; the wing tips flick away, saying no and no and in fact never. Eventually, they give up, standing angrily in the middle of the paved street between tents, watching as we vanish into the crowds. A harpy, they decide. An angel, whispers a small girl who passes by on bare feet and vanishes much the way we did.

This park has become home, though it is transient. All things are, in the end. We wander without fear, watching the other freaks and ferals as we often watch our selves. Fire, steel, blood, each of these things is consumed the way others would eat fruit, steak, berries. Nothing is surprising—not even the entire building that houses infants in small boxes that are said to grow them into properly sized people—though everything is captivating. Beast is calmed by the idea that there are such things in the world; Beauty clasps her hands together and frets until Beast unhinges them and holds one.

Beauty wants so much to be good, as good as the little girl who sits within a locked cage. Her mouth gleams with a thousand needle teeth, hands more like talons, but how this girl sits! Legs tucked beneath her, crossed at the ankles. Spine straight. There is no sign of the scale which runs a river down her belly and between her legs; a dress of white lace wraps her up perfectly. She folds her hands into her lap and keeps her teeth behind her lips even when she smiles. Beauty wants to be *this* magical thing, this animal reined in, trained, without flaw.

Beast wants so much to be awful, to unlock the cage and let the little girl tear her dress to shreds. The gleaming teeth should be shown to the world—people should count them and tremble; the talons should be unsheathed and used to tear the world asunder. The scale which brands her skin should be allowed to breathe under open sky; how it must look running with the river's waters, with the sun's light. That dress should be trampled in mud, until it is brown, earthen, gone.

Beast holds Beauty's hand, and in that heated whisper (please, oh please) Beauty hears a thing she cannot deny. Beauty will break open all the things, if only it will silence Beast.

***

There is no silence. Even in the dark with my eyes closed, I can hear the breath. I breathe in and out and match that rhythm, yet realize what I am doing. There comes a point when I can no longer separate me from the we, and there comes the night when Beauty cannot separate the need to be good from Beast's need to devour. One seems inherently like the other.

We stand upon our turntable, under the warm sunlight.

Today we wear white, not because we feel pure but because we wish we were. There is too much blood between us and Beauty says we must stop. But Beast demands.

Mister Hoyt watches us; we see snatches of our selves within his ceaseless glassy gaze as we turn and turn. His expression is furrowed today; there is a line which runs alongside his nose between his eyes, like a dry river waiting to be filled. We cannot tell if this is a frown, a scar, a line drawn with an ink pencil. We see a similar line beneath his jaw. He becomes a puzzle, fitted together in ways we do not yet understand.

Today we turn amid a thousand paper stars. Beth, who helps keep the circus fed with her sweet marmalades and warm breads, folded them with her clever hands as the train made its journey to this eastern shore. She said this star is what was, this star is what will be, and this star is the future none can know. We cannot have that future, because it's in the future; we want it now because we are a greedy heart, but it cannot be had. This is why we call it the future; this is why it is always now and never then.

We close our eyes and listen to the rattle of the paper stars as we move through them. Today, we have a mirror made to look like a nebula, painted with whorls of acrylic and oils; these colors begin to run down the white silk we wear, painting patterns of their own accord. We close our eyes and lift our arms and never find our selves entangled within the strings that suspend the stars; we are fluid and like them, distant, removed, something that can be observed but never possessed.

They all want to possess. One man steps past Mister Hoyt and reaches for us, touches the hem of our silk drape. Before he can get closer, before those sausage-fingers can wrap our ankle, he is pushed back into the crowd by our tender. We watch this man; he edges closer again and we bow our heads to get a better look. His eyes are black as pitch; his teeth stained from cigars. His fingers are coarse and stick to the white silk, his head bald and sprinkled with sweat within which we see the globe of the sun, the arc of the sky. There are no clouds.

He wears a gun under his jacket, strapped to him with brown leather. Our fingers long to slide under that leather holster, ease it off and know the tacky feel of his shirt. We suspect within his pocket we would find a badge, and when at last he comes to our tent to solicit our private favors indeed we do find a badge and indeed his shirt is tacky with sweat, with warmth.

"Need to ask you about a man and his wife," he says, and we don't know who put him on our trail, because who was there to tell? Someone—Mister Hoyt, ever lurking?—saw the man and his wife, watched them enter our tent and never exit. We make a low sound, something closer to a purr than a hum, and our fingers slide down his shirt buttons, steadily opening each. We cannot say where anyone goes once they leave this place. Beauty wavers. Beast breaks the last button. It flies toward the tent wall, and ricochets off to then furrow into the dirt floor like a bullet.

"We did not—"

Beast covers Beauty's mouth with a thin hand. Beauty's eyes meet Beast's, and then we look at the man before us. He doesn't look wary but drugged, like every other who comes to our tent; he is impossibly intrigued at the sight of us, wants to know what lies beneath our paint-stained silk. Wants to know how our breast curves and whether we are concave or convex in all the proper places. His mouth says either is fine, divine, sublime. Whenever anyone looks into our eyes, they fall through the brown and the gold and land in the black.

"We did not."

These are the only words, lies though they are. Beauty

carries a plea with every glance, but Beast cannot obey. Beast must suffer the gluttony

There are but two hands participating in this destruction, weakened yet resolute; Beauty caves inward while Beast gorges. *We need to stop; we cannot stop. We need to find another way; for us this is the only way. We need to stop. We cannot stop. Perhaps you need to stop, but you are not you; you are we, and we are starving.*

We fold his shirt and set the holster atop it when we are done. The shirt is dried of sweat now, crisp, and the gun smells like oil. His skin pools on the ground like empty trousers. We lick the blood from each other, slow like we are waking up and the carnival stands around us in silence. In truth, there is a tremor of sound just beyond the canvas walls. So too there is a small shadow. An eye peering through a tattered hole. Our breaths catch.

The old canvas tears easily beneath our hands, no talons required. Like the girl in her lace, we are unleashed from the tent's confines, streaking after the small form who flees, who saw too much. Its small feet stutter across the ground behind the tents, but then we have scooped it—her—into our four-arm embrace and she shrieks. This terrible sound vanishes beneath our mouths—Beauty has no hunger but knows that this secret cannot escape. We swallow ragged mouthfuls till we choke, till blood streams our chins, splatters our chests. Everywhere, we are flushed red with terror and anger and so too lust. It is a momentary glimpse of a hunt, a life we perhaps lived before we were bound into this shared flesh.

We destroy, consume, and cough it all back into the grass. When done, there is nothing left that resembles the young child who peered through tattered canvas. Perhaps five strips of skin splay as a hand might have, but no—no, we will not see that. There are only our shaking hands, fluttering wings, and a screech flying from our mouths. What have we done? Not what we must. Beauty pulls, claws, pummels, but cannot escape Beast.

In the warm dark, at last we rest. We do not touch; we lay as still as we are able, arms crossed over chests, wings carefully folded beneath. There is one breath, because one other is held. Lungs flutter still; body waits, poised. And then a hand across a belly. Breath comes once more. Hitched this time, unmatched. Fingers slide down shared belly, between shared legs, and curl. Soft, as if saying come on come on. Beauty wants to go, wants to come undone, and Beast refuses, but in the end, cannot. In the dark, there is a gasp. Ours, as it ever was.

We twist amid a forest made of shining metal willows today, hand-cut by Foster, who always smells of metal, of money, and train tracks. Mister Hoyt has returned to watch us. He talks to us today as the crowd is thinner, less interested. His interest never wavers.

It is a simple severing, he says, and he gestures as men of the world do (with prejudice, with agency, with insistence), to the juncture between us, where waist dips into waist. Mister Hoyt wants to break us as he might a cracker, easily in two as if we were never one. We have but two legs, we remind him, and he dismisses this with a wave. One of you shall have the legs, and one of you shall have a construct. This is disagreeable, we tell him, and he gestures to the valley between our legs, eyes narrowing as the silk which wraps us folds and bulges by turn. *This* is disagreeable, he tells us. This is us, we tell him, and we vanish behind trailing metal leaves to emerge a moment later, wings unfurled. He steps back, cowed. The small crowd murmurs in wonder. Can we fly, they always want to know.

We tried in our distant youth to rocket our selves into the sky. We fell more than once. We tried from the ground, from a cliff, from the very tree tops. We bruised elbows, knees, wings. If I severed you, he tells us as we circle more trees, you could fly. But we would never be whole, we say, and our hands slide down our chests, across metal tree trunks and shining leaves, to make each shimmer. False tree, faux angel, he watches us and wants to break us. When he offers Jackson double for our time, Jackson does not deny him. We are beautiful and beastly and why shouldn't he receive double every time?

"Jabberwock," Mister Hoyt calls us when he circles us within our tent, as if he can still figure out how we are made, how we have been joined into one imperfect flesh. The lines upon his face seem eased today, but are there in memory. "Hell needs its angels, too."

His hands are fine and strong and they slide over our arms, over the braided confines of our hair. His fingers dig into Beauty, to send ginger hair spilling. He doesn't spill Beast, and later, when Hoyt is bent and broken upon the ground, Beast's single braid that flips down a bare shoulder gives him a hand-hold; Hoyt clings, pulls, until his hand spasms and opens, until it goes limp as the rest of him.

"'Twas brillig," we tell him.

We gyre and gimble, streaking the canvas walls with blood in our haste.

Park officials notice when Mister Hoyt goes missing—Hoyt was one of their finest fleshcrafters, they say; he would not simply leave without word when he had done such quality work within the carnival park's walls. The three-legged burlesque dancer; the bearded hippopotamus, the man whose every finger and toe tells the time in a different country, the miniature lady (aged twenty-seven) who can sleep in a teacup!

They question Jackson, ask of his company of freaks. Jackson is all cool denial despite the warmth of the day. The air carries with it the scent of tar; Mister Hoyt's new exhibit is close to finished, a place where people can ride boats through Hell itself and laugh at having escaped afterward. Hoyt wanted us to be a demon, the officials say; he came for us, they say, and now he cannot be found.

Once they have gone, Jackson comes again. It was never a problem, Beast's appetite, until we found our selves in this stagnant place, this world within a world, he says. Before, the train would come and go and our performances were fleeting, but now that we are the main attraction people flock to, our beautifully strange ways are more closely observed. Jackson will never, he says, lose us, let us go, abandon us, leave us behind, kick us out, but here—

he leans in, pulls our mouths close, and kisses us hard, his tongue forked between our lips

—here, he says, we must be more careful. We cannot do what we naturally must. In his eyes, we see all things: we see the train stretching ever out, across this land and others we do not understand; we see Jackson alone and surrounded, we see him bent and broken and young and tall; we see him leaving us (oh he said he would never) and we see our selves flying. You can fly if you show patience, he tells us.

Patience is not our gift.

We go to Mister Hoyt's Hell Gate because we cannot resist knowing. We walk through the illuminated buildings and into the dense red glow that beckons from the park's center. These bulbs have been coated in red paint and it throws everything, including us, into a strange glow. This building is larger than we guessed it would be, but then the underworld is large, vast. It must be, to hold all the dead. Its entrance is a yawning arch like a mouth, with a river instead of a tongue within; there are small boats to tightly hold two through Hell's journey. The air smells heavily of pitch here and the lights sizzle with warmth in the night's cool air.

Within the mouth of the gate into the underworld, we see the child. The child who watched us through the tent's canvas. Something lurches inside us, for this is impossible—the dead do not come back, no matter what stories say. Yet here stands this child, reassembled with clumsy hands; her leftover skin shows the trespass of not needle and thread but the imprint of broad, strong fingers. Behind her looms Hoyt, the lady and the lawman, and countless others. These dead have been remade.

Mister Hoyt does not wear his woolen suit tonight but stands before us naked, his skin a riot of lines that mark the passage of hands, blades, magic. Within this body, we see our selves: a being that is not necessarily male or female, a being that has been severed in two—the way he would have done us. A simple severing; we can hear the words echoed as his fine fingers stroke over the line that mars his hip, the line that once dipped into a separate waist. Behind him, we see that there had always been two. Here stands the other Mister Hoyt, the part he cut away, rising from hips and legs that have been constructed of abandoned skins, bones, lashed metal.

Beauty wants so much to be good.

Beast wants so much to be bad.

We dig our feet into the ground, and from our center we pull—we pulled this way in our youth, trying in vain to part our selves. It is no easier nor more possible now. We are a solid flesh, a thing that cannot be parted no matter how we think we wish it. One would have legs and one would have a construct, and this is as disagreeable as the Hoyts who stand before us. We approach him and our feet print the ground; the grass has not grown because of the construction; there is soft dirt and stones and the debris of building this Hell Gate.

The little girl fashioned from her leftover skin bolts at the sight of us. She screams and flees into Hell and the lady with her cigarette-burned thighs follows. The men regard us with even stares, but though dead, their eyes have not lost the sheen of lust for whatever it is we are. Angel or demon, perhaps we are not a thing to be named, all desires being equal in the warm dark. Even so, they withdraw, leaving only the Hoyts before us. The mister we have known smiles, mouth slightly crooked from however he has been pressed back together. He extends his hands to us; they are strong still but coated in blood and tattered flesh, the signs of his trade. Sometimes, he says, a thing must be sacrificed so it may properly live.

And who deems *proper,* we wonder. Mister Hoyt smiles again and lunges. Hell will have its angels—or its demons. Fine lines and distinctions, things we have never drawn but others always do. We turn our shoulder to him and our broad wings catch the brunt of his impact. Though these wings have never carried us into the sky, they are strong and living and bear him backward, toward the river which snakes from the mouth of Hell. His severed twin cannot move quickly at all; this Hoyt mewls pitifully as we stride past. This is what he would make of us? How he would separate and reduce?

We are accustomed to working quickly, within the shadows. We are accustomed to silencing our prey so that none come running, and we are upon Mister Hoyt before he can cry out. But Hoyt has been remade by his own hands—be they his own or his twin's. His crafted flesh is a thing we do not understand, for it comes apart beneath us. He seems many creatures in one, leftovers bound into a whole; they part, they scamper, they reassemble deeper along the river's path. We pursue the gleaming trails in the red light, the twin's mewling growing ever more distant.

Deeper, the halls smell of sulfur and of the hot glow of the glass lights. Mister Hoyt sucks himself back together and flees deeper into Hell's ever-branching caverns. He keeps to the illuminated riverbank, the freshly-sealed channel below ready to be flooded by the Styx. It is here, when he turns to gauge our distance in pursuit, that his remade body staggers into a row of lighted bulbs.

The glass shatters and there is a brilliant flare as filaments and shards rain into the fresh tar. There need be only a single spark—the tar comes to quick fiery life. The fire is faster than us or Hoyt; his newly crafted skin browns under the heat as though he is made of bread. The fire appreciates the lines which mark him, running like water to fill every empty valley.

The burning Mister Hoyt lurches into our arms, begging. While he pulled himself apart moments before, the fire seems to be fusing his flesh into a solid lump, now incapable of escape. His tongue can barely form words before a snake of fire slides into the open hollow of his mouth. He tries to turn toward the river, to fling himself into its watery salvation but there is no water to be had, nor salvation in Hell. We hold him even as the flames stretch covetous fingers toward our wings. No, we tell him, and while Beauty sobs, Beast roars.

Bit by bit, we feel our selves becoming ash. Small pieces of us lift into the inferno: skin, wings, a string of freckles once tongue-traced in the early morning quiet. Around us, the fire spreads along every fresh line of tar in the hollow of the river channels, deeper through the caverns like some far-ranging sea creature that will devour all in its path. These arms of flame surge through the entire park to ignite buildings, trees, tents. We can hear the screams and they sound so distant, but they are our own as the flames wrap us the way silk once did. They curl around our shoulders, our waist, to lick the cleft between, and tell us that sometimes a thing must die before it can live.

Beauty arches under the heat and tries to pull away. Beast crisps up, ephemeral dough, unable to pull with arms so withered. A simple severing, so simple, yet Beauty grasps a wasted hand that grasps in return, and pulls. Pulls us upward out of Hell and into the ashy air where we, as one trailing embers, fly.

LIMINAL

1880, SILVER RUSH COLORADO

I WAS ALREADY DEAD WHEN the train came, but still I heard that whistle. Felt the keening wail all the way into my bones that were no longer bones. I could feel, too, the warmth of the railroad track, beneath hands that were not my own. Gemma's fingers curled around the rail and the last rumbling of the cars rolled up her arm, into her shoulder, to curl around her neck like a scarf. Sombra reached for Gemma, hauled her easily into the car while the scent of old hay and animals rose around us. Horses, I think it was horses, as we three flopped there and waited for the train to lurch into motion. It did not.

I could feel myself breathing, though I had neither body nor lungs. Could feel myself shaking with exhaustion and cold both.

"I can't believe we left Honna—"

"Ssh."

Sombra shushed Gemma, closing a hand tight around hers. I felt both Sombra's squeeze and the shift of Gemma's hand under it. I listened to their combined breath, fogging in the cold mountain air, to the patter of the rain on the roof of the railcar, and to the crunch of booted feet over gravel.

"Don't take stowaways."

Sombra looked up and I focused through her ebony eyes to see the man who stood outside the car on the shoulder of the tracks. He was small, though rounded in the middle, gnarled hands holding onto a long stick. He had a kind face, cheeks rough with stubble, a bright blue cloth around his neck, like he'd stolen a piece of Colorado's autumn sky and tied it there.

"Stowaway implies secret," Sombra said, and I felt each word in her mouth as though they were mine. "Stowaway implies we don't mean to pay." The hand that didn't hold Gemma's unfurled to reveal a small lump of silver, still coated with dirt.

The man leaned forward and sniffed. Like he was smelling the metal. Could he do that? Sombra could. She could smell the metal even if it were buried a hundred feet down. Gemma could hear the metal, like someone had struck a tuning fork. I could taste it, even now as it rested in Sombra's palm that felt like my own and yet was not. *Was not* ... Could taste the dirt that clung to it, and the sweet silver beyond.

Confused, so confused.

Sombra crooked her fingers and the man snatched the silver from her palm. Her mouth parted in a smile, a smile which I felt and also saw through Gemma's bright eyes. Bright from tears; Sombra leaned into her to kiss them from her cheek and salt water burst across my not-tongue as my not-cheek felt them kissed away.

Men were the same the world over, Sombra thought. They could be charmed by money if nothing else. But this man, he lifted his eyes back to Sombra and Gemma, taking in their tattered clothing, their cut arms, their tangled hair. He looked beyond all that and saw something that made me suck in a breath.

Sombra, I thought, he knows something.

Sombra *heard* me. She lifted her hand and rubbed at her ear, as though she were trying to dislodge an errant fly. I buzzed again.

He knows something!

My elder sister shifted in the hay as if she could get away from me, her skirts sliding up to show a pale length of plump leg. The man, strangely, did not look at that. He was fixed on her eyes, holding her black gaze.

"Don't take fools, either," he said, and slid the sliver into his pocket. "This here is a working train, and you'll be expected to earn your keep."

"We always do," Sombra said, ever practical. She bowed her head and though she was rain-soaked and filthy from a week at the end of a kidnapper's rope, she still had something regal about her. Something I had never been able to pinpoint. Her-my hand tightened on Gemma, who leaned in closer, offering the man a silvered smile.

The man nodded only once, then moved farther down the tracks, to other cars. Gemma's silver eyes followed him, widening at the sight of others gathered there. Strangers, with worn faces and clothes alike. The man tapped his stick on every train car he passed and every train car seemed to give him an answer of sorts. I could feel the hum of the metal on my not-tongue, could taste this old machinery, and underneath the rust, there was something sweet indeed.

It was the bridge that called to me and pulled me back, because that's where I'd met my end. They used to call it the High Pass Bridge, but now I hear they call it Three Sisters Bridge. After we three.

Those early nights, I would dream of it, and so Sombra and Gemma dreamed, too, tangled together on a thin mattress the trainman—Jackson—had given them. I remembered the wood of the bridge, slick with rain under my fingers. Sombra's own fingers curled in her sleep as though she touched the old wood, hard after countless decades in the weather. It had not splintered, but had become like iron after surviving the storms. Gemma's toes flexed as I remembered setting foot on the bridge slats. We'd all been barefoot, my toes had curled over the edge of one slat, watching the river far below. It was spring, and the rivers of the valleys were already starting to swell with snowmelt even though the days could still hold a chill to them.

"Come on."

Franklin Roberts had a sandpaper voice, every word sounding cut in half, like someone had taken a blade to his throat at some point. I couldn't see a scar if they had, though, but that meant little. Sometimes, deep wounds left no physical mark.

He tugged the rope which bound we three, taking our hesitation for fear, though it was more curiosity. We had seen this bridge before, but from the ground. To be up here was nearly a wonder. Roberts's St. Bernard pressed his nose against my leg before trotting out onto the bridge himself. A soft exhalation of warm breath and then he was on his way.

We didn't like what we could do, didn't understand it, but had taken men into the mountains before. Still, it had never been like this. At the end of a gun, tied with ropes, beaten and cut. But then, the world changed, a mother died, and men took advantage. Men took ...

The metal train car vibrated around us as the stick beat against the door. Sombra turned over and I watched the world shift around me as my perspective within her changed. Then Gemma moved and the scene shifted again. I saw through both eyes this morning, bright and dark both, a blur of shapes and colors.

"Up, you."

The train had weaved its way out of the mountains and onto the plains of Colorado. Small towns or no, people came to the carnival when the tents were set. Kids came to watch them pitch the tents, pointing to one and then another, whispering about what they might contain. I tried to move closer to the kids, to listen more, for it reminded me of my sisters and the trains. But whatever I was now, I was bound to move as Sombra and Gemma did.

There was a great clatter as cargo was off-loaded, a burble of delighted voices that seemed to say the train was staying awhile. Sombra and Gemma moved through the tents as they went up, feet barely seeming to skim the short spring grass, leaving a murmur in their wake as other members of the carnival got a look at them. Still tattered and bruised, but beyond that there lingered a mystery, a sense that each woman harbored something magical inside. My sisters' cold fingers caressed the sides of the train cars every now and again, drawing from the metal we had for so long wondered about.

Ever since I can remember, we heard the trains. We always dreamed of where they went and who they carried, having no good idea. We often thought our father had left us on a train, thought he might come back on one, too.

Mother said we didn't need to know him, that he was an angry son of a bitch from up north. She told us of our birth—the three of us together in the dead of winter, sprung from a drop of Father's blood in a circle of greenery that should never have been, and hadn't been since—we stopped asking questions. It was clear to us that Mother didn't want us asking, though when Sombra found a circle in the woods where nothing would grow and where animals would not venture, we all had to wonder.

Mostly, we thought about those trains. One might bring him back any moment, so we looked for that puff of smoke in the sky and the sharp whistle that could signal him.

A train never did bring him. Ended up taking us away, instead.

Jackson ran a tight train. He was a business man, first and foremost, a showman second, though it's possible only the slightest breath separated first and second, truth be told. He was good at what he did, and the people who traveled with him loved him for it.

Jackson had said we needed to earn our keep, but our talent was seemingly nothing that could entertain the masses who came to the carnival. He called Sombra and Gemma to his own train car one evening to see exactly what their potential was. I wondered if they would tell him what they were capable of. What we were.

The train car was sparsely decorated, faded posters on the walls, faded rugs tossed on the floor. A roll of tenting huddled against one wall, scarlet and cream, while a small desk sat in a green pool of light from a lantern. Jackson had a lockbox before him, a pile of receipts spread across the battered wood desktop. There was but one chair in the room other than that which Jackson claimed, blue and gold striped, but neither Sombra nor Gemma sat. Sombra kept an arm wrapped around Gemma, who was shaking. Gemma could barely lift one foot in front of the other to get to Jackson's desk.

Jackson looked them up and down when they came in, his eyes seeming not the least bit tired behind the half-moon spectacles he wore. His mussed brown hair needed a brushing; it looked like he'd been digging in it with his gnarled fingers. I tried to reach a hand out, to smooth an errant lick of it down, but couldn't guide Sombra's or Gemma's fingers that way. Still, Gemma curled her hand into a fist at her side, as if she were resisting. Sombra's hand shook. Was it harder for her?

"Surely there is some talent you possess," Jackson said, drawing his glasses off to regard them across the desk.

My sisters had cleaned up well. Gone were the tattered dresses they had come in; Miss Delilah Chase, a lady with a good deal more beard on her face than one might normally expect, had loaned them satin skirts and corsets, and while the corset laces were let out as far as they might be, Gemma and Sombra still looked quite the ladies. We had never owned such finery ourselves, and as they'd dressed, I had felt those laces under my very own fingers. Could feel the swell of breast and hip alike, and the slip of satin against thighs.

Gemma leaned against the desk for a moment, which steadied her shaking. Her silver-blonde hair slipped over one shoulder. "You might find many uses for us," she said. "Do any of your ladies share pleasures with the male patrons?"

Jackson blinked, as though such a thing had never occurred to him. I caused Sombra's eyes to flutter—I couldn't simply blink, it seemed. I was surprised by Gemma's offer and I think Sombra was, too. Once, our mother had been asked if she would rent our services—not those in finding metal—and she'd answered the man with her shotgun. Such things should not be given for any price, Mother said. Now, to have Gemma offer it so freely ...

Take it back, I wanted to scream, but it came as a rush of only air, air that filled the train car and ruffled my sister's skirts; air that blew across Jackson's desk and scattered every receipt there. Jackson tried to capture them, but the damage was already done. Whatever order he'd placed them in was destroyed.

As the pressure within the train car built, I could feel each side of the car as though I were pressed against each with hands and feet. Could feel the roof against my back as I bowed up. Near to exploding.

"H-Honna, stop it!"

I tried to stop, I really did, but couldn't. My anger burst out of me like a small tornado, sending every bit of paper into the air. The door to the train car flew open on a rusted track that squealed a protest. The light in the room slanted; the lantern on the desk toppled over, the wind from my anger extinguishing the flame before it could catch the rest of the oil and set the entire place ablaze.

"Honna!"

Sombra's scream deflated me. The pressure in the car eased and I felt only the floor then, as I curled around Sombra's feet, lost in her magenta skirt.

Jackson peered up from over the edge of his desk, hands spread in the debris of receipts. "Who ... is Honna?"

Gemma leaned into Sombra, curling her pale hands around Sombra's darker arm. Light and darkness, and me the air between them. "Our dead sister," Gemma whispered.

You might think a man would panic at that. Dead sister, here in the room with them? Responsible for the outburst that had ruined the small office? Jackson only grinned. It was a slow thing, calculating. I did not think then that this man was as kindly as he seemed. Oh, he could be, but deep down, he knew what his circus needed. Knew what the people would pay to see. And right then, that was us.

Jackson took his time with us, wanting to know exactly what we were. Trouble was, we didn't exactly know ourselves. The things we could do, we'd simply always done them. Our mother said even as infants we'd gravitated toward metallic items, rooting them out from even the ground when we were outside. Metal called to us. She was forever finding spoons under our beds, small coins planted in pots.

Metal still called to me, even though I was … not. I had no physical body left to me, and yet could still taste the metal of the train cars on Gemma's tongue as though it were my own. As though I'd walked up to each train car and licked it to fully know the taste. The red cars tasted stronger than the green; the little blue caboose tasted like the memory of a place I had once been but could no longer find.

Jackson wanted what Roberts had—the secret to our talent, but we couldn't give it, being that we didn't understand it ourselves. We didn't understand what happened to me, either. In the dark of night, when the train was at rest, Sombra and Gemma curled together in the dark and whispered. What had happened? Did Roberts do something to me? Where was I? They could both feel me, that I knew; they could feel me slip between them as easily as a whisper, filling up all the little spaces between and around. They tried to deny it, told themselves they were dreaming, but deep down they knew better. Deep down, they knew it was driving them mad.

I kept going back to the bridge. In my dreams, I carried Sombra and Gemma with me. Bare feet on rain-wet iron-hard slats. The dog's breath curling warm against my leg. Roberts pulling on the rope that tied us. Sombra and Gemma resisted, said now was the time—now, now, now!

And then they pulled. Pulled so hard we three went down on the bridge. The dog whined, breath coming out in clouds, then scampered off the bridge and away as Roberts charged.

"Come on!" Sombra screamed the words, pulling that wet rope, trying to get me and Gemma to our feet. But Roberts had hold of me on the other end, Gemma caught in the middle in this awful game of tug.

Roberts drew his knife, a hunter's knife that was well cared for. He was a hard man, in desperate need of money, but what he owned, he took good care of. That knife bit into the rope and as Sombra tugged, he cut. Cut until the rope came apart and I went staggering back into his arms.

There was a moment when he smiled. Beyond his wet beard, his mouth parted to reveal crooked teeth. But it was a joyous smile, as though he'd won something. My bare feet slipped on the bridge slats, I went into his arms hard and unbalanced him.

We flipped over the rail as though we had been pushed, and it was Gemma's scream that followed us down. It was a long fall; it almost felt like there would never be a bottom to the valley, and when there was, it was icy snowmelt that closed over us. Icy water and rocks and

then—

Then, I was back on the bridge, standing between my sisters, looking down into that valley at the churning river. I curled my hands around Sombra's arm and she shrieked. She batted at the air to push me away and screamed and screamed until her throat was raw. At long last, she didn't push Gemma away. Only curled against our sister and moaned like her heart had been ripped out whole.

That was when the train's whistle rose above everything, and we moved.

———

Jackson called Gemma to his train car, alone. I curled around her neck close to where her heart beat, tattered bits of me resting between her small breasts as she stepped into the ring of light nearer to Jackson's desk. He crooked his fingers and she came closer yet, as though he had her tied with a rope the way Roberts had. Gemma slipped around the corner of his desk, her skirts whispering in a low, emerald voice.

She thought he meant to take her up on her offer, of men finding pleasure with them, but when he finally took hold of her, she gasped in surprise. I felt the sharp draw of breath and the pain, too, where his fingers bit into her arm. He was quick about it, drawing a sweet-smelling kerchief from his pocket to press it over her mouth and nose. This awful, heavy scent made me withdraw; like clouds coming apart under hard wind, I felt myself dissolving. I slipped from Gemma's neck, onto the dirty floor, and pulled myself back together.

As Gemma finally slumped, unconscious, Jackson dragged her from the light, into the depths of his train car. There, against the back wall, were two cages, like one might keep animals in. Jackson opened the rusting gate of one, and pushed Gemma inside, before relatching and locking it. Inside, Gemma lay still like death, knees drawn to her chest.

I fled. I slipped through every crack that train car had and stretched long across the frost-tipped grass. Could see in my not-eye the bridge Roberts had pulled me over, could feel those cold, wet slats under my not-feet as we slipped and went over. Reaching for Sombra now felt like falling all over again, and I discovered then, she was gone, too.

The train car stood quiet, mattress empty, lantern snuffed. The scent of it did not even linger in the cold night air, so it had been awhile. I could see tracks in the dirt outside the car, bare feet and booted, but they vanished into the grass, the frost having covered them well.

All the long night, I looked. Looked but could not see or feel Sombra. I could taste her though; her fear coated these mountain woods and the back of my tongue alike, thick and bitter. It was nowhere and everywhere, and I could not latch onto it.

Knowing where Gemma lay, I crept back to her side, slipping through the cage bars. But when I settled beside her, she came awake, shrieking like she was being *killed*. Her hands knotted into her hair, over her ears, and she rocked, screaming incoherently. I did not want to leave, tried to touch her, crawl inside, but she bucked like a green horse, flinging herself against the side of the cage until at last I left, and her screams turned to whimpers carried on the night wind.

The following day was quiet. I could not go near Gemma without making her shriek and I could not find Sombra, so I shadowed Jackson. On the surface, his day was ordinary. He walked circles around the tents to inspect them and be sure they were holding up well under the constant tug of wind; he spoke with employees as to the evening's performances; he visited the few horses they kept and offered his hands to them to nuzzle with velvet noses.

But beneath that calm surface, I felt something else was at hand, and when he shuffled back to his train car, and a dog fell into step beside him, it seemed like a puzzle piece. The St. Bernard gave a low whuff into the evening air and I could remember what that warm breath felt like against my own leg as we stood near the bridge. Roberts's dog, now Jackson's?

What had Jackson done to my sisters? What torment did they know while he roamed his circus train?

Jackson packed the main tent that night, oversold the show and left people pressed outside, straining to see. Experience the Weird Sisters! his hawkers cried. Witness the Sheer Bounty of Strange!

I lingered at the top of the tent, against the striped canvas though it moved against me with every breath of wind. Prior to the show, the lights in the tent were doused; everyone there was thrown into darkness and Jackson let it linger long enough to grow uncomfortable. The people fell to utter silence, and then you could hear the uneasy murmur among them. What was happening? Could anyone see? Did something just brush against my leg?

The lights returned with a great explosion; from every corner of the tent, colored-glass oil lamps were lit in the same instant, bathing everyone in a strange, green glow. It seemed as though we were underwater, compressed by great fathoms of water. I stretched along the tent, my not-eyes riveted to the cages which rolled into the center ring.

Two cages, one draped with blue-dyed canvas, one of them the animal cage from the back of Jackson's train car. I could feel then Gemma's heart lodged in her throat. Warm and salty, metallic and not unlike silver. A thing that called to me, bid me down to the ground. I clung to the tent canvas, trying to feel Sombra in the other cage.

The fire that was my eldest sister had been banked. She existed—oh yes—but as a low pile of cooling embers only. I reached for her and it was like reaching my not-hand into an icy lake. Beyond the chill, there was a fiery sting, something that promised warmth but could not yet deliver. I drew back, attention rounding on Jackson, who walked between the cages, his walking stick having been replaced with a whip. I became aware of a low rumble at the base of Sombra's throat. Wherever she had been kept, she knew well the feel of that leather lash.

In the sickly light, Jackson appeared like a man from another world. His small body unbent and he stood straighter than I'd seen before—the showman in his element, garbed in a suit that shimmered in the green lights. He was not small and hunched over with pain in this place. His face unpinched itself and, though bathed in emerald and lime, seemed at the height of health. He smiled and lifted his arms and the crowd leaned forward as one, to see what he had brought before them.

"I beg you all to be witness tonight," he said, his voice carrying to even those outside the tent. "I beg you to witness these *strange* women, these *weird* sisters, and know them for what they are." Slowly, he rounded the cages; I could smell the ground beneath his boots, dirt that had been pounded by horses earlier in the day. "They are not human women, my friends, oh no. Not these."

The whip trailed with a whisper across the top of Gemma's cage. I felt her flinch as my own.

"Angry and strange, they will consume you if you look too long upon them." Jackson moved around Gemma's cage, to a point again between them, where a table had been placed. He set his whip to the side and drew back a blanket to reveal a staggering sight. "Two bodies trying to contain three souls! They must be appeased!"

The crowd drew back with assorted gasps at the sight of the struggling sheep bound to the table. Jackson took up a knife, not unlike that which Roberts had used to cut me free from my sisters, drew back the sheep's throat, and cut it open. My sisters screamed with the sheep, and it felt I did, too, until our throats were raw from it. Warm blood, a familiar metallic tang against my not-tongue, and to the west I could feel every bit of silver calling us. Burning into us. The blood flowed down the sheep's neck, over Jackson's hand, into a bowl of honey where it pooled crimson against the gold.

"Strange offerings for strange women!" Jackson cried above the din of the crowd. He was losing some of them—some of the more delicate ladies in the audience had swooned. Others had fled, pressing through the eager bodies yet outside the tent. These came in to take their places, to gape at Jackson's sacrifice in the ring. "I give you this, O Silver Sisters!"

There was a strange reverence in Jackson's voice at that, an almost-caress that seemed to slip right down our spines. Gemma curled into it, while Sombra leaned toward it and then, angry at herself for doing so, revolted. Her entire cage shook. A spark burst from Jackson's hands, and the sheep, blood, and honey were engulfed in flame.

Sombra came alive again; heat called to heat, and she drew this power into her. The blanket that covered her cage was wholly consumed by the flames; for a moment, it looked like she was sitting in the middle of the fire herself. I could feel her straining against the metal which confined her, and Gemma, too. I was drawn to that power, unable to fight it, and slipped away from the tent roof, riding those warm currents of fire toward my sisters.

Jackson withdrew; he stepped back and dropped to his knees, mindless of the pain they gave him, his eyes bright with tears as he watched the scene before him. I felt myself sucked into the heat of the flames, near to exploding again; felt whatever was left of me turn liquid and stretch, reaching for the cages.

The metal doors flew off their hinges, into the crowd which moved like some confined ocean wave in the tent. I was aware of a new metallic tang, fresh blood from the weeping crowd. Bodies pressed under hot metal doors. Seared flesh. Screaming children.

I stood again on the bridge, toes curled against the iron-hard slats of wood. Roberts's knife, bright in the rain, sharp as it bit into the rope. I clung to that memory, as though it might anchor me and save me from the madness in the tent. But I saw then it was also an anchor to Gemma and Sombra. If I didn't let go, they would never let go.

I let go. The tide turned black and devoured me. I channeled the blood and the screams and the fire and beneath it all, the sweet taste of that honey; sucked the power from them and reached for my sisters. Reached until my not-hands took hold of them and dragged them from the ruins of their cages. At that touch, the three of us together again, the tent exploded.

The striped canvas snapped upward, as though a great hand grabbed it. The poles came inward and the crowd fled, strange black shadows in that green light. Three days later, Jackson's boys would find the tent and its poles in a Kansas field. Tonight, there was only the fire from the sacrifice, the broken oil lamps that scattered the field.

There was something else then, a prickling along my arms, an awareness that I was once again sheltered within a body. Gemma's head rested gently between my hands, silvered hair trailing across my fingers and arms. In a blink, I shifted from Sombra's body, into Gemma's, and she was not screaming, but welcoming me inside. I watched through her eyes as she looked up at Sombra, her body seeming black like the night sky above, strewn with stars. Charred by the fire, yet still alive. Still alive

...

"Sombra?" Gemma whispered.

"Hush now," she told me, and gathered the Gemma-me against her. I bled out of Gemma and back into Sombra, feeling securely held between both. Sombra lifted her head, eyes pinpointing Jackson. Blood and soot made a strange mask over his face and Sombra nodded to him once. "Thank you."

These were not the words I expected her to say and only in the days that followed did I understand. My thought that Jackson had known ... the sight of the St. Bernard trotting at his side ... the discovery of a stack of bills in our train car, tied with a slip of paper that read "Roberts." Sombra and Gemma sat with this money between them one evening, legs crossed Indian-style.

"He knew," Sombra told Gemma, black eyes lifting from the money. Her fingers moved over the stack of bills between them, sparks of fire glinting from their tips. "He heard what we were and claimed us."

As much as this should have horrified Gemma and me, it didn't. Gemma nodded, stardust shifting down her shoulders. "Broke us and remade us right," she whispered, feeling *right* for the first time in years.

Roberts hadn't wanted silver at all. He'd hunted us at Jackson's behest. In the end, though we escaped Roberts, we had still come to Jackson's train, drawn by those often-heard whistles that carried through the mountain valleys we called home.

And now this train was home, my sisters and me remade into something we had never imagined. My sisters were two halves of the same thing, one light and one dark, and me still the breath between them. Where one was concave, the other was convex. Where one was sharp rocks, the other was smooth water. Sombra's hair was the night sky while Gemma's was the stars. And sometimes, I made them exactly backwards from that.

BLOW THE MOON OUT

1957, PHILADELPHIA

In those moments before, in the dark of the woods, we were near perfect likenesses of each other: faces round and curious, not having lost the plumpness of youth; eyes brightened by the possibility that lay at the end of our journey; coats buttoned up proper and bags carrying all we thought we needed still neatly zippered closed.

One might look at we four and say sisters, but we were not. Beneath our exteriors, we were as different as sun and moon, as Earth and Mars. Each might hang in the same sky, but one burned with its own light while the other could only reflect what was thrown its direction; one exploded with water and life while the other hung as a dry husk, millennia dead.

Moon was what my mother called me, bundling me like a crescent within her arms as she rocked me to sleep on the back porch night after night. Her weathered hands smoothed over my cheeks as she told me there was no man in the moon, but a girl, round and plump, gleaming pale as moonlight itself. Moon was what I was, then—in those moments before.

I didn't possess my own light, but readily reflected and studied that of others.

1. Strays

The woods were not lovely, though I would grant them both dark and deep as we wound our way closer to Philadelphia to see Jackson's Unreal Circus and Mobile Marmalade. It was the best of all possible worlds: Halloween had come and gone, but the weekend stretched ahead and with it, a chunk of treasured, unsupervised adventuring.

My sister Audrey, seventeen, slim, and perfect, had kicked us out of the faded tomato-red Rambler still on the Jersey side of the river. She was supposed to take us straight to the circus, but left us before we'd even hit the old rail bridge. It wasn't right, but after seeing the empty look in her eyes, none of us said a word. We slid out and she was gone almost before the door latched shut. We would end up like the boy in the box,

Norma whispered, but Trudy slapped her arm and for a long while we stood in silence, daylight running out around us.

Two nights ago, Audrey and I sat at the very intersection we shuffled out of now; the Rambler rumbled as it always had and Audrey stared down the road, like she could see all manner of things I couldn't. She pulled a pack of cigarettes from her purse, held one unlit between her lips, and just stared. *Joel wasn't supposed to ... he was supposed to be there, supposed to take me, Lucy.* The cigarette had bobbed, drawing a long shadow over her chin, her neck. In the half light of the streetlight, she was just shadows. She never did light that cigarette.

Four shadows stretched across the road now as we nodded at each other, resolved, and left the pavement for the woods trailing along the Delaware River. Five miles to the bridge? More? I didn't know, had never been there on foot before, and wasn't sure why Audrey had been.

The Delaware River growled a distant rumble to our left. The day was not yet over, but sunlight struggled to reach the ground here, leaving the mulch dappled in vague shadows. I placed my foot in every slight mark Rum left ahead of me, as she followed Trudy. I glanced over my shoulder to make certain of Norma. She was still there, though lagging behind, the tall grass plucking at the frilled hem of her skirt.

"They are *not* putting a dog in space."

Norma, who tended to cringe every time she heard a male voice, cringed now, even though there were no boys or men close. Her head came up sharply at Rum's words. Her eyes were as dark as the woods, but I could see the confusion in them. I looked forward again, to the set of Rum's slight shoulders, to the bounce of Trudy's copper pompadour turned umber in the forest gloom.

"Lu, you tell her—dogs don't go in space. *People* don't go in space, tell her."

I kept pace with Rum and Trudy, but also held my silence for a minute. The Russians had a bomb stored up for every man, woman, and child in America. Why wouldn't they shoot a dog into space for kicks?

"They're doing no such thing," Rum said again around the gob of chewing gum in her mouth. "No one would put a dog in outer space, for crying out loud. What good's a dog gonna be up there? Not like they can do experiments—"

"You aren't listening to me, Rum. They can *be* experiments," Trudy said. Her own gum sounded like a sharp gunshot as she chewed the air out of a bubble. "They're going to see what happens to the dog, right? Next step, probably *people*. In *space*." She lifted her hands into the gloomy air and wriggled her fingers, the silent explosion of a billion rockets. While provoking the others seemed like a thing that gave Trudy glee, there was more to it than that. I had seen the way she blushed when Norma looked at her. It was the same way Audrey blushed when Joel looked her way.

"God wouldn't like a dog in space," Norma muttered as she came up alongside me, like there was comfort in being closer. She jabbed her hands into her coat pockets like they were faces and she was punching them in. "If dogs were meant to go to space, they would already be there. God put them on the ground for a reason. Just like we're on the ground. A *reason*."

Rum's shoulders bowed a little. Then, she turned around and walked backward, eyes on me all the while like I was the only known spot on a map. Her face was round and trusting, a cherub, dark hair hanging in glossy ringlets against her cheeks. "Lu, you tell me, they wouldn't put a *dog* in space ... would they?"

Rum was a year younger than us, thirteen. She claimed she was a runaway from the Amish in Lancaster and while we weren't sure how possible it was—we had never seen any black

Amish—we couldn't disprove it, and Norma had tried three times. I alone knew her name wasn't Rum—it was Hannah Fisher, a thing she'd sworn me to silence about.

Rum didn't have family anywhere local, that was for sure. She had lived at the children's home with the nuns for a good bit now, but the world remained exceedingly strange for her; everything was horribly possible all at once because she didn't know any better. Maybe shooting dogs into space was a thing.

I was the one she asked; even above the sisters at the school, she trusted my word, even though I was a writer, and skilled at making things up. Especially stories where people, dogs, and insects went into space on ships named *Presley* and *Haley*, and loved it there.

"They're Russians, Rum," I said. "No telling what they'd do." I pictured my sister sitting with her unlit cigarette, remembered the flutter of her pulse in her throat as she sat and stared into the night. *Joel wasn't supposed to ...*

Rum's gaze swung back to Trudy. Waiting. Trudy nodded and stopped walking, to shift her pack into her hands where she could unzip it. Inside were crammed magazines, their paper and ink scent sharply filling the evening air. We each stopped in our tracks to wonder at what was in there. I felt some things would be certain: magazine covers of Elvis, newspaper clippings about Paul Anka, her transistor radio that she likely smuggled out.

"Sunday morning, going to shoot her straight into the stars," Trudy said. "See here." She might have been a librarian with the ease her fingers found across the magazine spines and edges, to pluck a rumpled newspaper free. Mars Bars wrappers crinkled in its wake.

Rum's hand shot out to take the newspaper. Such things were still small miracles to her, she who claimed to have run away from her folks because she refused to be married. I supposed if people could catapult a dog into space, other people could try to marry off their child of a daughter. Amish were much like Russians in my head; as alien as the creatures I spent hours writing about.

The story about the dog was made suddenly worse with the unfurling of the newspaper. The dog had a name, an image, a set of bright eyes that one could get lost in. I refused to look overly long at the grainy image, but Rum couldn't look away.

"Laika," Rum read. "She was a *stray!*" Her eyes shot up to Trudy who only nodded again, justifiably smug now that she had produced newsprint evidence. Rum scoured the article, assuring us she would read only the germane bits, which seemed to be every word on the page. They were launching the dog into space on Sunday, to study the effects of space on a living creature.

Rum's shoulders sank and she started to walk, eyes still riveted to the paper. I elbowed Trudy as she zipped her bag shut, but it was Norma's voice that filled the long silence with reprimands as Rum walked away.

"Just a stray—still a creature of God, like Rum if you think about it long enough. Runaway, stray, not much different. What do they think's going to happen to it? The dog, not Rum."

"Nobody knows," Trudy said, and they both fell back into step behind Rum. "That's the point."

I followed, but slower, because my mind was coming up with all sorts of things that could happen to that poor dog. Asphyxiation. Alien abduction. Rocket could fall into the moon or back into the ocean, gravity depending. Rocket could fall apart before it even left the launch pad and what of the dog then? Mostly, I wondered if we Americans would try to shoot the rocket down, thinking it was a bomb, thinking that we were going to blow them up before they could blow us up.

We walked in silence until Norma started singing "Sand-man." "Bum, bum, bum ..."

One by one, we chimed in. It was a song we practiced for no good reason—"because we could" didn't seem to please our parents enough. They found us silly as we tried to harmonize the way the Chordettes did, but mostly we didn't care. Singing to the mythical Sandman brought its own rewards, even if the lyrics were ridiculous. Trudy refused to sing beyond providing the "yeees?" when the Sandman finally appeared; said it was degrading to dream only of a man, which made Rum kick it up even higher.

"And lots of wavy hair like Lib-er-ace!" Rum fairly hollered as we walked ever toward the still-distant bridge in the growing dark.

The dog came out of nowhere. It was like the darkness peeled a part of itself away and lunged for Rum. Later, Trudy would say the dog didn't want her singing, either, but mostly I think it was on account of her being loud and small, seemingly easy prey, but for we who closed in (after a good stretch of mindless shrieking, make no mistake).

Rum was on the ground before I knew what had happened, Trudy and Norma leaping back, stumbling into trees and each other. I stopped altogether, staring at the twist of dark forms in the growing dark of the woods. I couldn't tell Rum from the animal at first, didn't even know it was a dog until I swung my bag and caught it in the nose. It reeled back with a whine and I grabbed Rum by the arm, pulling her out of biting distance.

She was so still and quiet, especially in the wake of Trudy and Norma screaming at the dog. They chased it into the trees and I hauled Rum into my lap, trying to ignore the way my thighs shook, the way my hands were covered in blood from where Rum had been bitten.

"Ohjesusohjesusohjeeeesuss."

Rum was not given to prayer, despite being roped into a covenant school, nor was I. Oh, we all went to church every Sunday, and sat proper and listened to words that were supposed to encourage thought and reflection, but mostly we wanted to be tromping through the woods, setting up forts, brushing out each other's hair, making firm denials that any of us were growing up ever. We were not curving in new places, we were not asking our mothers to buy us bras or feminine hygiene products and the world was still one long, continual summer afternoon where anything but these strange things was possible.

"Get your coat off," I said and my voice was strangely thick, like I had been crying and yelling and I wouldn't admit to either.

I helped peel Rum's coat off to see the blood well up from her forearm. "Jesus Christ," I bit out.

The screams in the woods grew more distant, the crash of undergrowth and fallen branches and who knew what else. I reached for my bag, the zipper hard to work with bloodied fingers, but eventually got it open. I grabbed the first thing I came to, rolled knee socks, white, splattered with purple polka dots. They were my favorite, a birthday gift from Audrey. I unbundled them and tied each one tight around Rum's arm, paying no mind to the way she hollered.

"We are going back," I said, and made to move away, to get her coat and my bag, but Rum caught me before I could do anything.

"We are *not*."

I could picture a hundred things going wrong with Rum's arm. It could get infected. It could bleed itself dry and wither right off at her elbow and when it dropped off, the dog that bit her would be there to pick it up in its awful maw and carry it away for dinner, for a toy, for a trophy.

"Makes no sense going back," Rum said. "Just like it makes no sense to shoot a dog into the moon. Into space. Wher*ever* she's going." Her voice dropped low and her fingers uncurled from my arm. "We're not going back. Wrap my nightgown around my arm. Put my coat back on. They don't need to know. I need to go."

They would know, I thought, but I opened Rum's bag, found her nightgown (butter yellow with a tiny pink ribbon rose at the neckline), and wrapped it around my socks which already bound her arm. We stuffed her into her coat with grunts and groans and by the time Trudy and Norma came back, breathless and sweaty, we had washed ourselves clean with the water from Rum's canteen.

"Don't know where it went," Norma said. She bent over, hands on knees as she tried to breathe.

"Away is good enough," Trudy said. She glanced at the sky, then back down to Rum. She laughed. "Maybe Laika's spirit crawled into that dog, came to tell you she wants to go, huh?"

"Spirits don't work that way—dogs don't even *have* souls. Spirits certainly don't crawl, what do they tell you in that church of yours," Norma began, but Rum cut her off with a "bum, bum, bum, Mr. Sandman!"

Norma threw her hands up and stalked into the woods, back on the path we'd been keeping to as if there had never been a dog, a chase. Trudy hefted her own pack and gave me a wide smile before following her. I gave the still-singing Rum a hand up from the ground and we followed.

"German shepherd?" Norma asked once the singing had settled down, and the dark rose more firmly above us. We would have to stop soon. "Bloodhound? It was big. Smelled bad. Like it had been out here a long time. Saint Bernard?"

I hadn't noticed any smell, but I hoped the dog hadn't been sick. It was too easy to picture Rum getting sick, turning green or purple or some other hideous color as her body began to rot. Maybe she would turn into a dog and then there'd be no hiding it.

Behind us, I heard a sound like a dog walking through leaves. Crunch, crunch, pause, crunch, snuffle. I looked back, but it was too dark to see anything. I rooted in my bag until I came up with my flashlight, then shone it on the path behind us.

"What's there?" Rum asked.

I had turned to walk backwards, still shining my light behind us. "Nothing," I said, just as my light skimmed past a pair of eyes that lit up like small, exploding suns.

We screamed.

This only set the dog off, digging paws into the earth to charge us. God, it was huge. I wanted to brain it with my flashlight, but kept hold of it against all instincts shrieking otherwise. The light bounced through the trees as I ran; falling stars, ricocheting headlights, the sunlight in a wavering mirror.

"Into the trees!" I screamed. "Into the trees!"

The trees weren't made for climbing, but we did our best with what we'd been given. The bark bit into my hands and knees, and by the time I'd gone as high as I could go, I'd wedged the flashlight in my shirt, in the slim strap of my bra where it crossed between my breasts. First thing it had been good for.

I pulled the light out and aimed it to the ground, searching for the beast. It was there, making circles around the trees. It was huge, didn't look like a proper dog at all. Drool gleamed down its jaw, ceaseless as it stalked us. It didn't bark, only cast its gaze upward, watching. Waiting.

I shone the light into the other trees, looking for the girls. I found them one by one, clinging as I did to a branch that seemed only just wide enough to not break right off. Rum's eyes were wide with terror, Norma's, too, but Trudy, she was laughing as she wrapped herself more tightly around the tree.

"Now there's a dog that needs to be in space," she said.

2. Gently Down the Stream

It was probably a Saint Bernard, but hard to say.

Come morning—a Saturday that was trying to rain, when we should have been in our own homes, having syrupy pancakes—Rum and I were still in the tree tops, the dog sleeping beneath us. It was possibly white at one time, but had been so long in the woods, it was now the color of the woods themselves, blotchy brown and gold and black. It had no collar, so no tag.

Rum was in the tree closest to me and she was the color of old, dried mud. She was shaking as she tried to hold on to the tree and maybe this wasn't going to end well, but surely it had to end soon. I looked for Trudy and Norma, but saw no sign of them. Had they already climbed down? I looked back at the dog. Had it eaten them? A thing like that, you'd think we might have heard it.

"Rum, we need to climb down," I said.

"There's a ... There's a dog down there, Lu." She yawned and I could see how paper-dry her lips were.

"There is not a dog down there," I said. I adjusted my bag, checked the flashlight in my bra, and began to climb down the tree. "There is a fairy trapped in the body of a dog—a fairy who doesn't know any better than to plow into four girls who're walking to the city to see the circus. What does she know about anything in that body?" I paused on the next too-thin branch, listening to it crackle. Rum hadn't moved. "Let's find out, Rum. Come on, climb down with me. Bet you can't beat me."

That was enough to get her moving. I exhaled and said nothing more as we moved down from the trees. No branches broke; I found if I moved fast enough, they just didn't have time. When my feet touched the ground, the dog lifted its massive head to look at me, but didn't move. Its eyes were chocolate brown, curious but not hostile like last night.

I moved toward Rum's tree, to clasp her by a foot and help her down to the ground. Like my mother would have, I pressed a hand to her head, thinking I would be assaulted with a veritable book of information about what ailed her. No such book came, but I was certain she felt warmer than she should have, especially with the misting rain.

"Here." I uncapped my canteen and handed it to her. She drank like she'd never had a sip of anything in her life. I wanted to unwrap her arm and take a look at it, but also didn't, because that meant admitting we had a problem bigger than a dog possessed by a fairy.

"S'fairy?" she asked, wiping her hand over her mouth.

I nodded and looked at the dog. "Only explanation." Of course there were a hundred others, though the dog didn't look sick. I crouched down to study it and its ears perked forward, tail worming through the damp leaves. "Maybe she's forgotten how to talk—given that drooling mouth, you can't actually blame her ..."

There was an empty wrapper near one paw and the dog's tongue lolled out, to curl around a tattered chunk of Mars Bar. Leaves came with it, but the dog didn't seem to mind, swallowing everything in one gulp. The tail scrabbled in the leaves again, happy, eager, dog-like. I couldn't quite convince myself it was a dog, all things considered.

Rum had crouched down beside me and tipped forward to her knees, to bend almost entirely to the ground as she studied the dog.

"Laika?" she whispered.

The dog's entire body wriggled, but it made no move toward Rum. This was not Laika; it bore no resemblance to the dog in the paper. As Norma said, souls didn't work that way and Laika was in Russia, getting ready to head to the stars. Whatever this was, it wasn't that. This close, the dog did smell weird; syrup, shaving cream, and chocolate.

Rum whispered, "Free, free, a trip to Mars, for nine-hundred empty jars. Burma-Shave," and reached a trembling hand out.

"Rum, I don't think you should—"

The dog's tongue spooled out again, this time around Rum's hand in a slobbery lick. Every part of me was poised to jump at her and haul her back, but the tongue withdrew without taking her hand off. The dog leaned forward and Rum scratched it between its eyes.

I stepped backward, into Trudy and Norma who had returned. Their arms were full of sticks and rocks, and I helped them clear a space to make a small fire. Norma ringed the rocks, I tented the sticks, and Trudy pulled a magazine and a lighter from her bag. She tore pages from the back of the magazine, carefully along the spine edge. Only the advertisements, though even this left the first couple of pages loose. She tucked them carefully away before setting fire to the pages balled under the sticks.

"Here."

Norma offered up a bag of marshmallows. This kind of thing was tradition; when our parents let us go on a weekend, we were on our own for all things. While we had pocket money for food and circus admissions, we had packed a good many things we weren't normally allowed to eat. Root beer and melted marshmallows for breakfast, for example. Trudy passed out bottles of Hires, but not even that was enough to get Rum to join us.

"Dog didn't do anything when we climbed down," Trudy said as she leaned a bottle of Hires against the log for Rum if she wanted. She then skewered a marshmallow on the end of a stick and held it into the flames. "Gave him a Mars Bar though, just in case."

"Dogs shouldn't eat candy," Norma said.

"Well, he did eat it." I glanced away from Rum and the dog, back to Norma with her strict set of rules and Trudy with her distinct lack of them. In the humid morning, Norma's curls had turned into a brown cotton ball while Trudy's pompadour curved almost flat against her skull.

"Found a cardboard box out there," Norma said. "Flat, wet."

No one said anything to that, but we were all thinking the same thing. That poor little dead boy the police had found, that no one stepped up to claim. Wrapped in a plaid blanket and just left there. Left in a box. Dead, dead, dead. I burned my tongue with my marshmallow and took a long swallow of root beer.

"How far are we?"

The question came from Rum. She pulled herself up from the leaves and came to sit by my side. The dog padded alongside her, flanking me. It looked at our staked marshmallows and then back to Rum.

Trudy palmed her hair out of her eyes. "Not too far, few more miles up the river to the bridge—"

"The *rail* bridge?" Norma asked. "We can't cross there—that's for trains."

"Might as well cross there—no sense in walking five more miles." Trudy twirled her marshmallow in the flames until it was a dripping black mess, then brought it to her mouth.

Norma hunched her shoulders in her coat and let her marshmallow catch fire; it dripped into the sticks, long strands of white instantly blackened.

"And what about this stupid dog?" Rum tried her best to sound angry about it, but somehow didn't. She also didn't sound scared. I think I would have been scared, having no good idea about the dog or the wound it had inflicted.

"It doesn't seem in a hurry to leave." Trudy lobbed a stone toward the dog's paws; it landed short and the dog didn't even spook.

Even as we smothered the fire and packed our bags, the dog stayed with us, and once back on the trail, it loped slightly ahead, as if leading the way. I tried not to think too hard on that, worried about Rum. She didn't look any worse, and was walking as normal as anyone, but I couldn't forget the blood on her arm last night or the muddy color to her cheeks this morning.

"Well, did he put his arm around you?"

Ahead of me and Rum, Trudy and Norma walked with shoulders nearly together, but at this question, Norma took a step away.

"He did not," Norma said. "Once you let a boy put his arm around you, he knows exactly how far he may go. He wanted to, but ... no. He did not."

Trudy pressed. "Did *you* want him to?"

Trudy was forever wanting to know about boys, about dancing and holding hands and arms scooped around shoulders. She dreamed of kissing, no matter that everyone told her if she turned her gorgeous fall of copper curls into a pompadour, she would never be kissed by a boy ever. She didn't seem too upset, only wanted to know about kissing. The news that Norma had been within touching distance of a boy who wanted to put his arm around her was special indeed. I hadn't been kissed. Trudy hadn't been kissed. Rum said she never wanted a thing to do with boys, which led Trudy to believe she had been kissed and often. That our rule-following Catholic Norma had been so close to a boy was revolutionary.

Norma didn't answer Trudy and Trudy laughed. Laughed so loud she startled birds from the wet trees. Norma shoved her and walked a little faster down the trail, arms clasped around herself.

"That wasn't very nice, Tru," I murmured, but Trudy only laughed more.

"No, it wasn't," she agreed.

"Bum, bum, bum," Rum sang, but no one joined in just then.

We walked in silence and eventually Rum's hand slipped into mine. She was tiring and cold from the rain that never quite fell. The sky was a sheet of gray beyond the trees that were half-empty of leaves. It seemed we should have been to the bridge hours ago, the woods stretching out impossibly far. I questioned how far we had actually gone and glanced back only to see endless woods on that side of us, too. The birds had gone strangely quiet and so had the river, as if we were farther from it and the bridge than we ever had been. Where had Audrey left us? A shiver slid down my spine and when the dog barked, I nearly jumped out of my skin. My hand tightened around Rum's.

Above us, high above the canopy of trees, a dark shadow circled. This had caught the dog's attention, setting him to barking and capering farther down the sodden trail. I couldn't tell if it was excitement or annoyance, but he didn't stop barking as he tore off the path and into the trees. I stopped walking and Rum, still clinging to my hand (or did I cling to her?), stopped, too. We looked up and watched this strange shape trace paths in the sky.

It was too big to be a bird—unless it was a vulture, but even at that, I had never seen vultures here and it was bigger beyond that. But it moved like a bird, wings dipping down to propel itself higher against the gray sky.

"What is that, Lu?" Rum whispered. "Another fairy?"

I squeezed her hand and started walking again. "Absolutely. You saw how the dog reacted." I looked ahead for the dog, but saw no sign of him. Still, I heard him barking. "Clearly they're related. Maybe she's come to pull the fairy out and put things proper." Maybe she could look at your arm, I wanted to add, but didn't, because again, that meant allowing we had problems and there were no problems here, nope.

Proving me right about our utter lack of problems was the revelation of the river and the shadow of the looming rail bridge ahead. I felt more than a little relieved at the sight of both; even Norma and Trudy looked comforted by the bridge's old, black bulk.

Beyond the tangle of half-bare trees and gray-stick shrubs that clung to the riverbank, the bridge stood stark against the gloomy sky, latticed iron bracing the longer girders. It looked drawn onto the sky with watercolors that were beginning to run to the color of rust, of time. The iron was supported by columns reaching into the water where they were encased in old stones; even from this distance, I could see they were colored with moss, lined with grit where the water had constantly licked past. Down the bridge's center, the railroad tracks which would guide us to the Philadelphia side.

"There's something ..." Trudy bravely picked her way closer to the river. She lost her footing part way through, and grabbed a low tree branch to keep herself up right and out of the cold mud. "People? There are people down there. Wait."

We didn't exactly wait. We came to Trudy's side, stepping

through leaves and mud to look ahead at what she had found. Trudy shushed us, but we had already fallen silent.

Down the riverbank, where the stones and pylon anchored the bridge into the ground, there huddled a group of people. At first glance, they looked like an extension of the wood's underbrush, half-dressed in leaves and half-bare to the uncaring sky. But as my eyes grew accustomed to their shapes, individuals made themselves known. A twig was an arm; a trunk was a torso. I counted a dozen different forms, or maybe there were fewer; it remained strangely hard to tell, but the important thing remained true: they were gathered around another form that floated in the river.

It was too big. Big and small in the same instant, deflated and drained of everything. A discarded Halloween costume, I thought, that's all it was, but none of us could resist in getting a closer look, not even Norma who proved true to her Catholic roots when it came to her fascination with the dead and all that accompanied them. Eyes on a plate, thorns around a disembodied heart, carry on.

I was certain it hadn't ever been human, but the way it spread in the water, it recalled a thing that had been human and no longer was. Its fingers were too long, trailing out nearly like tentacles, some curled around the dried weeds of the riverbank. If it ever wore clothes, they were long gone; the body pooled pale and utterly flat on the river's surface. It shouldn't have been flat; it should have bloated up, with water, with disease, with *something*, but it was like a sheet of plastic that a person could peel off and shake dry.

The worst thing was the face. Being that flat, you think of *nothing* like a face, until you start to look at it the way maybe Picasso would, with disgorged eyes and malformed mouths. It still had its teeth in its mouth (mouths, oh god, there was more than one), but these were also somehow flat, screams pressed into a book for safe-keeping. The memory of a nose, colorless eyes. Male or female, I couldn't tell and it didn't matter; whatever shape might have given it form was just gone. *Deflated.*

Among the mourners that ringed the body sat the dog that had accompanied us. He tipped his head back, howled, and then bolted out of the water, scattering mud and water up the bank.

Rum swayed and I wrapped an arm around her to keep her upright. Norma clutched Trudy's sleeve, and we all four hovered there, not daring to breathe or do anything that might bring that dog back to us. We didn't want them to see us, no matter the cold water that seeped its way into my loafers, creeping ever up my socks.

They lifted the body from the water and it came up like plastic wrap from the molded gelatin salads our gran liked to bring over. The body made a sucking sound and resisted, like it didn't want to peel away. Suction from the edges—where it clung most desperately to the water—made ripples course through the skin, if it *was* skin. These ripples smoothed out the more the people pulled, the body going so thin I could see the water through it. Norma's shoulders pulled tight, inching toward her ears until I thought she might swallow herself.

"Enough."

At this single word from a man in the group, the others let the body go. It slipped back to the river with a sigh. Norma nearly deflated, too; the breath she let go sounded like a sob. She buckled to her knees and we all reached for her.

"Norma—"

"She shouldn't have gotten up," Norma sobbed. Blindly, she clutched at us, tears streaming down her red cheeks as she kneeled in the cold river mud. "She s-shouldn't have ... She should have stayed d-down, let it hap—happen and pass the w-way the r-river ..."

We all knew—people talked, but not us. We never questioned, never wondered aloud, it was a known fact. It wasn't our place, but it could be. Norma was like any of us, raised in a household with siblings, with a mother, with a father. There were rules; every person had their place and lines were not to be crossed. Dogs didn't go into space—women didn't overstep their boundaries. The hard part was knowing where those lines were; understanding the boundary of water and earth was easy, other things less so when they changed at a man's whim.

I wanted to touch Norma's shoulder, to let her know it was all right, that though her mother had been torn and flattened by her husband's hands, it didn't have to be that way. But touching Norma was crossing the boundary erected around her by father, by brothers.

The shadow in the sky returned, but this time skimmed low to the water. It was a bird, I saw, but also a woman, and I felt something inside me stir at the sight of her. She flew across the river, filling her mouth with water until at last she alone could scoop the body from its wet mooring. The body came away effortlessly, cradled in the water of the bird's mouth as she lifted into the sky. She dipped under the shadow of the bridge, then up and up into the clouded sky with a hundred smaller birds in her wake. It was then the clouds broke, rain streaming coldly down.

The figures left the river and we withdrew, too, to the meager shelter of a thin tree where we settled Norma and let her cry herself empty. We wiped her knees clean of mud and pressed a root beer into her hands and without a word resumed our walk to the bridge. The circus wasn't far now.

The dog waited for us at the mouth of the bridge, paws wet and muddy. He shook himself once, then vanished onto the bridge, as if trusting us to follow. Maybe it *was* a fairy trapped inside, I thought, because what else could explain such a strange creature? Maybe, maybe, maybe it was Laika after all, eager to see what the circus had to offer before she took to the stars.

"What's today?" Rum asked as we set foot on the railroad ties where the rain beaded.

"Saturday," Trudy said. She rummaged through her bag to pull out her radio. "Saturday and the whole of a circus before us."

Saturday, and Laika goes tomorrow. Tomorrow.

"I hope they have c-cotton candy." This from Norma, Norma who had never voiced a hope before, only the cold facts she'd been raised with.

She had never tasted cotton candy, I was certain, and made equally certain to be sure that if she wanted, Norma could eat her weight in spun sugar before we left the circus grounds.

3. Idle

The bridge was old, built so long before any of us had been born it seemed to me a relic that should have been at the bottom of a sea somewhere, gathering moss and turning into a coral reef. It was sturdy as anything, but that didn't keep the wood from creaking under our feet as we made our way through. Latticed iron arced above us and provided just enough of a roof to make the Everly Brothers that crackled from Trudy's radio echo all around us.

Trudy sang along, following behind the dog, who followed Norma and Rum. I brought up the rear, suddenly hating "Wake Up Little Susie," because it made me think of Audrey waking up in a place she shouldn't be waking up, of her dark profile in the Rambler and the way she never lit that cigarette.

Joel wasn't supposed to ... he was supposed to be there, supposed to take me, Lucy.

Joel had been a part of our lives as long as I could remember, a grade or two ahead. He lived five minutes away from our house if you took the back way to get there, over fences and across lawns to bypass the dead ends and cul-de-sacs. Audrey took the back way a lot, sneaking out after we had been tucked in, swearing me to secrecy. I followed her twice. The first time, she'd met him in the park and spent an hour making out with him under a tree. The second time, they had taken off in the Ford Fairlane his father had bought him, sleek and black like oil running down the road. The car came back with windows fogged.

Sometimes we liked him, sometimes we didn't; he was popular, got good grades, pleased his parents at every turn, and had a headful of golden hair like any Greek god might. What wasn't to like, Audrey often asked. Usually, I couldn't be fussed to remember when we were supposed to like him and when we were supposed to hate him, but I was sure I wouldn't ever forget the first time he made Audrey cry, or the way she eventually stopped crying and just held that cigarette between her lips. Waiting for something that never came.

It was a regular part of life, waiting for things. Waiting for school to start, waiting for school to stop, waiting for the new Elvis song, waiting for the weekend and the cocktail parties our parents would often take us to, waiting for breasts to come in like they were something on order from the department store, waiting for cheekbones to pop out, or blood to flow so that we might actually Become Women, or ...

He was supposed to be there, supposed to take me, Lucy.

We all knew what it could mean, if you waited for a thing and it didn't show up. School always came, whether you were ready or not, but blood wasn't quite so constant. We had been told what it could mean, if the blood didn't come.

"... when they say *ooo la la* ..."

Either thing held its own amount of terror, bleeding or not. Audrey held my hand the first time, told me how things were supposed to go. I thought of her profile in the Rambler and wished I had held her hand, because I was beginning to think a thing I didn't want to think at all. The nights she snuck out to be with Joel, the nights she didn't come home till early in the mornings. I couldn't remember when they started going steady, Joel had just always been there. Until he wasn't.

"Maybe they were circus people," Rum said from the head of the line when that awful song finally finished. The dog barked as if it agreed with her. "Was just like a piece of wet paper, wasn't it? Didn't fall apart though. Maybe plastic."

Plastic, that body in the water. I swallowed hard, thinking about bodies and blood and the way that body hadn't seemed to have a drop left inside it.

"Maybe," Trudy said. "Here."

She had turned around, to walk backward while she extended a pack of cigarettes toward Rum and Norma. Norma's first inclination was to shake her off—the pack moved toward Rum, who took one, and then Norma, to everyone's surprise, reached for one, too. Trudy's mouth quirked up in a grin and she tossed one back to me. I caught it before it could hit the narrow shoulder we walked on.

We had to stop to light them and the dog walked in impatient circles around us as we did. The tobacco was dry and it crackled under the sudden warmth of the lighter flame. Norma took a hard pull on hers and doubled over coughing. Trudy slapped her on the back and then we were off again. I didn't actually smoke my cigarette; the smoke made my nose wrinkle. Rum lipped the end of hers like it might bite her, and spit out tobacco flakes, while Trudy attempted to show Norma exactly how to smoke without choking. Mostly, it seemed like an excuse to get close to Norma and watch her mouth around the cigarette butt.

Eventually, I flicked mine through the bridge lattice and into the river below. It vanished into the water without a sound.

"Does that happen to bodies? Often?" Rum asked. She picked tobacco from her tongue and made a face that set Trudy to laughing.

"Wasn't natural, what happened to that body," Norma said and Rum's eyes flicked to me, silently questioning.

I nodded in agreement, though maybe it was just a kind of nature we didn't yet know. Who's to say? Much like the Russians, there was plenty about nature we didn't know.

Coming out of the bridge on the other side, the Pennsylvania side, it seemed like everything should have been different, but it wasn't much. Another tangle of woods, though this time we moved away from the river and train tracks, setting up camp a short way in so that we could have lunch. There was bread and Kraft Singles and a fire set up to combine into toasted, melted perfection.

The problem with walking so long in the woods was having to eventually pee in the woods. Being that we were all girls, it wasn't so strange to wander off a ways, so as camp was set up, I wandered. Our canine companion had also wandered off and so did Rum. I watched her vanish safely behind a bush, then turned to find my own.

My own was already occupied, by a tall, hairy man.

But for the filthy hair, he seemed naked, naked and peeing in a bush, and I opened my mouth to say something stupid like "excuse me," but nothing came out, nothing at all. Despite that, he heard me, maybe my feet in the leaves or the way I sucked in a breath and made to choke like I was still holding a cigarette.

He looked over his shoulder—his eyes were brown and kind and startled—and his cheeks flooded with color and before either of us could say a word, he was just gone. He ran and I let him go, standing there, still needing to pee very much.

I managed, shaking all the while. The idea that he would come back, jump on me, and drag me into the bushes was foremost in my mind. I held a roll of paper in one hand and my flashlight in the other, dragged warm out of my bra where my heart still pounded like it was going to war. I would brain him. I would take him down before he could take me. Why was a man peeing in these woods, for the love of—

"Lucy!"

I couldn't say how long I had been gone, but they were hollering for me. When I got back to camp, Rum poured water over my hands so I could wash, and I sat near the fire to rub them dry. Trudy offered me a cheese sandwich, but hesitated before actually giving it to me.

"Looks like you saw a ghost," she said, and I shook my head, but knew I had to tell them.

The dog padded up to Rum's side as I told them about the man peeing in the woods. From that moment on, some of the joy went out of the lunch, because we were all on our guard, watching the trees around us. Was he alone? Was he hunting with friends? Were they out roaming the woods looking for girls to abduct? The dog, seeming to pick up on our moods, whined and paced a circle around us and the fire.

"Probably shouldn't stay here too long," Norma said. She shoved the rest of her sandwich indelicately into her mouth, chewing more than she comfortably could. Although I wanted to laugh, I didn't, because her point was sound. Much like the dog in the woods the day before, we had no idea what or who else was out here.

As we packed camp to go, our mood stayed low, quiet. Our eyes were never off the woods for long, and I felt suddenly foolish for taking part in this journey. I wondered if this was what growing up meant. Never knowing what was around the next corner but fearing it would be something I'd be incapable of dealing with or explaining to anyone other than my closest friends. No one would believe that body, or that man, or even this dog who still padded alongside us as we packed, smothered the fire, and left.

Worry ensured that we made good time through these woods; soon enough, the dirt paths turned to paved roads and signs of civilization began to assure us that we were getting closer to our destination. When at last we could see the city rising against the gray sky in the distance, I think we all blew out a breath of relief.

"It's like that on all the outer planets of the system," I said as we walked, our steps still quicker than normal and still that stupid dog at Rum's side like it was trying to apologize for nearly taking her arm off. She looked better, but not so much better that I had stopped worrying.

"Not so many people, right," I continued, "so when you turn a corner and find another person, there's that moment of shock, that instant when you don't recognize them as a person at all but something hostile in your space, something that means to stop you from where you were actually going. Doesn't matter that they might be just as shocked to see you—they probably are, might welcome a hello or a drink after the places they've been, but mostly, it's that heart-hammering fear that they're going to turn on you, or come back after they've run away, and do you some harm."

Everyone stayed quiet as I told the story—maybe it calmed them as much as it did me. Not the content of the story itself, just the sound of a voice that has something to share and knows where it's going. Fiction was like that. Point A always led to point B. Real life wasn't so much like that.

"Jupiter's the best," I said, "because it's the biggest and because of the clouds. Picture all that low-hanging fog, no other soul in sight for months. You'd just be a speck up there, like a grain of sugar tossed into coffee. So tiny. If you didn't melt, you'd surely be all squashed and rounded on the edges, rolling through fog, all alone till— Hello, what's this, another person? Edges all rounded off just like yours, but still strange because you'd weigh twice as much up there, maybe more. You both probably look like squash in the end and it's not like you'd be able to run, weighing that much, so maybe you'd roll away in your surprise, and then—Well, Red Spot, right?" I smiled now, carried away with the idea. "Probably a hole, straight to the middle of the world—"

"And what's inside?" Rum asked.

"Oh, more clouds. Always clouds."

"Like cotton candy," she said. "Falling forever."

Neighborhoods made themselves known as we walked; clusters of houses and stone tenements that rose along the paved streets. Rain glossed the streets and made everything look like one long piece of licorice, stretched beyond all its means. The deeper into this neighborhood we wandered, the first thing that hit us was the smell—it was popped corn and burnt sugar, roasted nuts and rain-wet animals.

But among the cars that lined the road through these gloomful tenements where only the occasional light glowed from a window, sat a car I knew, a car we all knew, the faded tomato-red Rambler, and though we walked past, my eyes fixed firmly to it. It was empty, windows rolled shut against the rain, but there was Audrey's discarded cigarette on the dashboard, and the dent in the driver's side door where I opened the door into a tree the first time Audrey let me drive, and the rounded corner of the small green sticker we'd never been able to get off the windshield glass.

In the building behind the Rambler, a small light burned in one window, but the door was shut and it was no place I knew. A sign beside the doorbell directed people to the back entrance.

The other girls didn't pause—I don't think they looked at the car, because they were so intent on following their noses to the tents and booths that sprawled through a space that had once been an empty field. It was muddy now, meager grass stomped into the mud that had come with the rains. Undaunted, countless people frolicked within the temporary fence that ringed it all. The entrance gate was staffed by two figures, each so extraordinary they drove Audrey from my mind.

The first was a woman who towered as tall as the entry gate itself. She was the largest person I had ever seen, and felt as though she possessed her own gravity; we were drawn in by her, to her massive figure which was given shape by a corset of burnished copper. Black layered skirts and a blouse frothed from either end and did little to disguise the ribbons of indigo ink that marked the giantess's skin. She plucked money from those who entered and the dollars seemed small in her hands, hands that could have easily gathered all four of us into one palm.

The creature by her side was something I had no words for. It was one being, two bodies that merged into one at the waist. They wore dark trousers to make this clear—there was but one set of legs—one torso clad in red, the other in white. Wings flared up behind both bodies, the straight fall of ginger-red hair interrupted by braids of black ribbons throughout. I could not say until I passed them by whether the wings they wore were real or part of their costuming, but after obtaining tickets, and stepping through the entry gate, the warmth of those feathers brushed my cheek, and I knew. If ever I lived on Jupiter, I would remember that brief touch.

Inside the circus grounds, we all started to change. Looking back, I suppose it wasn't a thing that happened gradually; it was swift. Probably we had started to change the minute Audrey kicked us out of the Rambler and made us walk, but only inside the circus did it become more evident.

Trudy seemed to glow and Norma stood straighter than she ever had before, like her shoulders were no longer bowed by some awful weight. Rum kept her hand in mine at first, but I could tell she was more confident, too, her nose working overtime to take in everything she had never smelled before. She was also due a good gorging on cotton candy, I thought, but the more she ate through the day, she changed all over again.

With everything she consumed—pickles, cotton candy, and bag after bag of popcorn—Rum seemed to get a little slower, a little more muddy around the edges. She tugged her hand out of mine to better hold her cup of soda, but I could see the way her fingers crumpled the paper cup, like she still couldn't quite get a grip on it.

When Norma and Trudy stepped up to the Ferris wheel to ride, Rum shook her head, said she couldn't do it. I stayed with her on a bench, watching the other girls wheel up into the cloudy sky.

"Let me see your arm," I said, even though the words stuck in my throat like dry toast.

Rum refused and when I reached for her, curling a hand into her coat sleeve, she flinched, then flung her soda at me. The top popped off and I was doused in dark, sweet cola. I'm not sure who was more surprised, Rum or me, but Rum bolted from the bench without her bag, fleeing into the circus with a cry.

"Rum!"

She vanished into the crowds, probably an expert at doing so, given she'd run away from so much in her life. Didn't have to be the Amish she had run from, but the girl knew how to cover ground. Lest I lose them, too, I waited for Trudy and Norma to come down and told them Rum had gone. Showed them her abandoned bag as if that was proof, when her just being gone was proof enough.

We each had watches, so made sure they were synchronized before parting ways. We could cover more ground this way and meet back up at the Ferris wheel when the hour struck. If we hadn't found Rum by then, we could do it again, and again. The circus wasn't without its limits, I told myself as I stalked through the muddy grounds. Of course, she might leave those limits, might wander deeper into Philadelphia, a city I knew as little about as I did the Amish. She might get hit by a bus. She might encounter that stupid dog again.

That stupid dog. I stopped in my tracks when I realized I had lost track of the dog. Had it come into the circus with us? I kept an eye out as I wandered, loitering by the steak on a stake booth for a long while, thinking the dog might try to get some meat. But there was no sign of it, and my hour to search was growing thin. I walked a slow circle around the outer layer of tents, the Ferris wheel in sight all the while, but there was no dog and no Rum.

I turned back to the Ferris wheel as rain began to fall more earnestly. I wished I'd brought an umbrella—of all the things to forget—and was wondering if they had any for sale as I stepped into the shelter of a tent. The tent smelled like damp straw and wet dog and I turned, thinking to find that Saint Bernard, but it was the hairy man who'd been peeing in the bushes. He was dressed this time, in jeans and a shirt that was somehow too well-pressed, and walking toward me. My mouth gaped open and I made to move, but felt frozen.

"Don't run," he said. "Please don't run."

Once, I would have run. Now, I started telling myself a story in my head, because one didn't just encounter the same hairy man twice, not without him following or stalking or—

"You bit Rum," I said.

At that, he stopped walking. His face seemed a mixture of dismay and guilt and he scrubbed a hairy hand across his mouth, as if he could wipe the expression away. He was still the color of the woods, browns and golds, and his eyes—they were the eyes of that dog, chocolate and desperate to explain. I clutched Rum's bag a little closer.

"Didn't mean to," he said and glanced at the crowds which passed us by. He took a step closer to me then, so close I could smell his wet ... fur? Hair? He smelled like he'd been rolling in the woods. "Sometimes ... I get *so* hungry, and Thurmond was dead and I was carrying *all* that grief, and there were animals —*girls* in the woods, and I just ..." He covered his mouth again, eyes closing. I didn't know if he was going to cry or be sick. "I'm sorry about the bush. Couldn't keep my form anymore, needed to breathe, needed to p—But where is she? Is she getting sick? I need to help her."

I didn't know if I was going to cry or be sick, either. I just stared at him, trying to understand anything that was happening.

4. Night Like a River

I launched into him and he let me pummel him. I hit him as hard as I could, confusion over everything pouring through my balled fists. Rum's sickness and Audrey being close for no reason that could be good, and this man who thought he was a dog, and Norma's parents and Trudy's longing for her. Everything came out and by the time I finished, I was sobbing, inconsolable as he had me sit on top of a bale of straw. He shushed me and tried to wrap an arm around me before he thought better of it and simply patted my hands, never quite letting them go. The touch was both alien and comforting. He was *so* warm and the rain had chilled me.

"Take me to Rum. I need to see her."

My head came up and I stared at him. I was still shaking, like my body didn't know what to do with itself in the wake of the anger.

"Take me to—"

"You're telling me that you're a *dog*?" I spat the question at him. I threw his hands off of me, no matter their warmth and slid to the edge of the bale. I wanted to walk away, but there was no way my legs were carrying me. "How crazy do you think I have to be to believ—"

"Stalked you in the woods," he said. "Rum was the smallest, even with that coat on. I wanted to tell you—when you found me in the bushes, but ..." Color flooded his cheeks, no doubt hot. "Well. I couldn't. I figured that *here*, here I could get her what she needed."

"And what does she need? Other than a proper doctor to tend her—"

"Proper doctor won't be any help." He stood from the bale and a shudder ran through him, shaking every bit of hair that sprouted from his skin. "I don't mean her harm. Any *more* harm. Blast it."

He walked away from me, pacing in slow circles. He kept trying to convince me, but he didn't have to. If he was that dog —and why couldn't he be that dog? It explained a lot of things— then it made sense, him knowing what needed doing for Rum. And I was being an idiot to delay things, because she wasn't well.

"I don't know where she is," I finally said when he paused in his pleading. He stared at me like I was the crazy one now. "She ran off when I asked to look at her arm—her arm which you bit and made her bleed and who *does* that, dog or not?" I came off the bale now, striding toward him. "How dare you stalk us in the woods?"

His chin came up and he bristled. I've seen cats get fluffy but never dogs. Dog-people. His lip curled to reveal his teeth, but he didn't move. Only nodded at me.

"It was a thing that happened," I said eventually. "Can't change that. Can only change where we go from here. Is Rum ..." Oh, my writer's mind was running now. "Is she going to change into a dog? Like you? Is her arm going to wither up and fall off? We need to find her, whatever you think is going to happen—and how do you mean to help her? You have medicine? A way to keep her from changing?"

To keep her from growing up. To keep all of us from growing up and being Audrey sitting in that dark car, the cigarette dangling from her lips. *He was supposed to be there ...* Joel hadn't been there for Audrey, but this guy was here and he was stepping up. Doing what needed doing, even if I didn't know what it was. I looked at my watch.

"I'm late for rendezvous," I said. "At the Ferris wheel. We split up to look for Rum." My eyes narrowed and I lifted Rum's bag toward the man who claimed he was a dog. He didn't question me, only bent his head and took a long smell of it. His eyes never left mine; it felt like a challenge—*prove it, I will so prove it.*

With Rum's scent in his nose, he grabbed my arm and launched us back into the circus.

The circus felt twice as big as it should have been, containing three times as many people as it did when we arrived. But me and the ... dog? ...cut a path through the crowds like they weren't quite there. I noticed we had support from up above, too; there were two forms flying above us, one smaller than the other, both black against the darkening sky. How hard could it be to find a sick little girl, I wondered. But then Rum was experienced at both running and hiding and I felt like my heart would break if we never found her again.

She would be missed at the children's home—she probably already had been missed, not getting permission to run away for a weekend ever, and that idea was like a knife in my gut. I clung to the dog-man's hand, terrified we wouldn't find her, but outside a tent that claimed to contain the country's only living mermaid, he stopped and took a deep breath.

I didn't have to breathe to know Rum was here. The small body that vanished into the tent was familiar by sight alone; the scrap of butter-yellow nightgown that peeked from the cuff of her coat was like a signal flare. I tugged the dog-man after me, after Rum.

She was so intent on her destination, she didn't hear us. We followed her into the tent, past the fabric wall that divided it into two spaces. Within the second space was a gloomy tank of water, illuminated by a bed of strange stones in its bottom. Rum reached for the water tank like she didn't know what it was, and maybe she didn't. Her hand trembled as she pressed it to the glass.

A face swam out of the gloomy water, vicious and astounding in the same instant. If it was a mermaid, I couldn't say; it was a woman, though, of flesh and scale and flowing green hair. Her webbed and clawed hand reached for Rum's, pressing against the other side of the glass. They looked like strange reflections of each other, Rum growing wavery like she was also underwater. Her knees buckled and the dog-man released my hand to catch her before she could hit the ground.

He carried Rum to the circus train, where it gleamed under

the rain on the tracks that ran behind the field. He kicked the door to the caboose open and through the unexpected scents of oranges and yeast, I followed him, watching as he lay Rum on a padded bench. The space seemed like storage and a kitchen both, full of cupboards that bulged with strange things. I thought I saw a jar full of fractured rainbows and another packed with tiny, tiny red-brown hearts, and a thousand-thousand jars besides, but mostly my focus was on Rum and the way her breath rattled in her mouth.

"Have to get Beth," he whispered to me. "Stay here."

There wasn't anywhere else I would have gone. I sat beside Rum and took up her hand in mine. She was clammy and hot, and I pulled her coat off so I could unwrap the damp nightgown around her arm. I expected it to be soaked with blood, but it was mostly sweat I found. The bite on her arm hadn't healed though; it was raw and red and angry as anything. It hadn't started to sprout hair or anything. I threaded my fingers through hers and bowed my head. I didn't pray, only hoped for the dog-man to get back here.

When he returned, he had a woman with him. She was instantly part of this place, and it was as if the place knew her, breathed easier with her inside of it. I could not explain the sigh of breath I heard, only knew it did not come from any of we four.

Beth kneeled beside the bench and reached for Rum. My hand came up to block hers and she looked at me curiously as our fingers brushed. Her eyes held something I couldn't understand, but her expression relaxed and she nodded a little.

"Just want to hold her hand," Beth said and drew her fingers back from mine.

I drew back, too, watching her take up Rum's hand. Here, she shook her head.

"Not her time," she murmured. She withdrew and turned

to rummage through her cupboards. "Probably going to be changed, but ... Here, take this."

Beth pushed a jar into my hands. It was filled with a coiled braid of hair, black as the stormy night that descended above us. Beth told me to wrap Rum's arm in the braid, but sliding it out of the jar was unlike anything I've done before. It was alive, slimy under my touch, pliant like my fingers pressed into a fish belly and not a length of dry hair. I retched while touching it, the scent of death and dirt beginning to fill the caboose.

The dog-man caught the jar before it could fall to the floor. My hands were filled with the strange braid and I found myself biting my bottom lip, struggling to wrap the thing around Rum's injured arm.

"And this. Pour it over."

Before I had even finished, Beth was giving me another jar, forcing me to wrangle the braid into some kind of order—was it my imagination or did it struggle as I tried to fold it around Rum's arm? I grit my teeth together, tucked the end of the braid into itself so it would stay, and took the second jar.

It was marked "angel tears," but it seemed more like sewer water. It was cloudy gray and filled with bits of eggshell, branches, seeds. I uncapped it and the smell of honey poured out. There should have been a wetness when I poured; the liquid should have run straight through the braid, but instead it clouded up like fog, streaming light so bright I had to look away. Beth hooked a finger into the lip of the jar and reclaimed it before I could empty it.

"And this, Dean."

The third jar was offered to the dog-man. He looked at it with revulsion, but uncapped it and drank the gray liquid down. It wasn't liquid against his mouth, either; as I watched, it turned to ash, threatening to choke him. Dean retched, bowing his head close to Rum's hand. The thick paste that poured out of him smothered the bright cloud, sank into the braid, and bound the entire thing to Rum like a cast.

"Now, we wait."

Joel wasn't supposed to ...

He was supposed to be there.

Supposed to take me, Lucy.

My limit on waiting ended. I couldn't, Audrey pressed against my heart like it might explode. I ran from the caboose, the back steps slick with rain. I slid down them more than walking, pushing past Trudy and Norma who were running toward the caboose (and did their lips look swollen from kissing and kissing and kissing or was it a trick of the stringed lights that had flickered on all over the circus?), and running toward the entrance gate. There were as many people as ever, but they parted like water for me and it was only when I'd hit the paved street again that I realized Dean-as-dog was with me.

He didn't stop me, so I didn't care that he came. I ran until it felt like my lungs would burst, until I reached that street where Audrey's Rambler sat. I feared that it both would and wouldn't be there. If it was gone, she was done doing the thing she had wanted to do with Joel ... if it was there and she wasn't yet done ...

But it was there and she was hunched over the steering wheel, sobbing the way I had sobbed inside the empty tent with Dean. I pulled the door open, not caring that I startled her, and reached for her. She slumped into my arms and clung to me the way I never thought she would, and there was blood—so much blood. Her pants were dark, but stained darker down her thighs.

At the sight of all that blood, I froze and for a long while, time seemed to spool without end. We would forever hang between all that had come before and all that should have followed behind. If I couldn't move, we were stuck. But the sun and the moon were never still; they were often eclipsed, but always emerged from those shadows. And how big those shadows! Surely this one was not so terrible.

But it was Audrey. It was my sister. It was a shadow that had weight and pressed me down until all I could feel was the warm shaking of her against me, until all I could see was the blood soaking her pants. Blood that should not be. This was illegal, we had been told time and again. This was why you didn't let boys touch you. This was why there were no kisses or dancing unsupervised. This was why you dressed like a proper girl, so that boys weren't tempted. This is why you didn't get into a car with a boy. Every single lecture was hollow in this moment. When Audrey looked up at me, her face creased in pain, I knew nothing was so simple as we had been told.

Big and small in the same moment, deflated, drained of everything.

"Lu, I c-can't. J-Joel isn't ..."

"He isn't here," I whispered, "but I am." I pulled her from the car as gently as I could. Audrey had a coat draped over the backseat and I stuffed her into it. I belted it closed and kept her in my shaking arms as we shuffled up the street.

The circus wasn't far, but it felt like forever. I didn't know if Beth could help Audrey the way she had helped Rum, but knew I had to try. Dean, even as a dog, didn't argue with me as we headed back that way. He loped ahead of us at the entry gate and the giantess and angels let us pass inside like they knew us. Audrey was cold and shaking by the time we reached the caboose and she grabbed my arms, shaking her head.

I guided Audrey up the caboose steps and into the warm strangeness of that room where Beth bundled her up, said it wasn't her time, either, but that she had nothing more to give me but marmalade. And when Beth pressed that cool jar into my hands, radiating a strange orange light, I just stared. Beth walked away and closed the door behind her, and I looked at Trudy and Norma and sleeping Rum, and had no clue what to do.

It was like this in stories, I told myself. A person is given a thing and just doesn't know what to do with it. They either took the thing firmly in hand and did what felt right, or they denied it. But what felt right? How did a person ever know?

I turned from my sister and friends and started rooting around in cupboards and drawers. I needed spoons, but failing that, anything to scoop, and in the end there were no spoons, only rainbows that flopped over when we held them and long sticks of spicy cinnamon that we all shied from. In the end, I poured a handful of the orange marmalade into my palm and no matter how strange it seemed, fed it to my sister. She swallowed it down with a grimace and I turned to Rum and did the same. I filled Trudy's palm and Norma's palm and then my own again and like we were drinking shots of booze at a party we had snuck into, we downed the marmalade.

With my eyes closed, it didn't taste like oranges. It tasted like grit, like a far-away red planet that I would never quite walk on, but would still know my way around. It tasted like Jupiter and a moon that vomited water into space, of clouds and the memory of Audrey holding my hand; like the first time I dived into a pool and got water up my nose, and Audrey hauling me out. These strange things calmed me, told me that one way or another, everything and everyone was going to end up where it needed to be.

"Tastes like beer," Norma murmured, and I cracked an eye open to look at her, wondering exactly how she knew what beer tasted like.

"Tastes like Norma," Trudy said, and got Norma's elbow in her ribs for the effort.

There came a sound then, a low groan that was almost a

growl, and I thought Dean had come back, but this sound emanated from Rum, who had started to twist and turn on the bench, as if caught in some terrible nightmare. We three reached for her and in my panic, the marmalade jar fell to the floor, shattering. Glass and sweet oranges made our footing slippery as we sought to anchor Rum; the harder she bucked, the more we slipped.

"She's g-going." Rum sputtered the words and I didn't know what she meant, not until her hand closed into my sleeve and she pulled me down. "She's g-going to d-die."

Audrey, Audrey, Audrey, my heart beat.

"L-Laika," Rum whispered. Her eyes rolled back into her head—I could see only the whites of them as she struggled to form more words. Spittle flowed from her mouth, as if she were sick or possessed or both. "Going now. Rockets. F-fire. Clouds of fire. There she ... there she ... g-goes." Rum's body arched up, as if an unseen hand had grabbed her by the waist. We clung to her so that she would not be taken, lost, but when at last she screamed and reached for something we could not see, we fell back and could only watch.

The Rum we knew fell away, but it wasn't the way I always pictured it being in story books. She didn't shimmer beautifully from one being into another, but rather one was ripped away to replace what she had been. Even the cast that Beth had applied to her arm broke off and tumbled away. The girl who loved running and found amazement in the things we found common was gone. In a splatter of blood and skin, she was gone, swallowed up by the creature that clawed its way out of her— looking not so fierce when all was said and done, for it resembled nothing so much as a tiny poodle, confused as to how it had come to be inside a caboose that smelled like spilled orange marmalade and blood.

No one said anything. We all sat there, looking at each

other but mostly looking at Rum who wasn't Rum, but a dog the way Dean could also be a dog. And then, an eruption of conversation, me trying to tell them how he'd bit her, them angry because I hadn't told them, and how did a person turn into a dog anyhow, and how could she have known Laika was going up right then and well, Trudy managed to reason as the argument lulled, Russia was in a different time zone and maybe it was already Sunday there, and Norma screamed that it didn't matter, dogs didn't go into space and girls did not turn into dogs and when they finished, Norma was crying in Trudy's arms, Trudy's eyes locked to me.

"Tell us a story, Lu," she whispered.

As if a story could banish what we'd seen.

Rum pressed herself down into the bench and licked the marmalade from my hand. I exhaled a low breath and reached for Audrey with my other hand. "Things never go the way stories say," I whispered, "but I'll tell you a story."

5. In a Barrel at Sea

The story I told Trudy and Norma was a story about four girls (sometimes five), who weren't girls at all. The whole night through, they hovered between Here and There, the caboose seemingly removed from both life and death, suspended the way orange peel was in marmalade. Because of that, inside the caboose things weren't entirely real. Things could be said there that couldn't be said anywhere else.

Had someone turned into a dog? That was okay, because bodies did strange things we couldn't always explain. Messy things, things that made us want to vomit. Had a girl kissed another girl? It was okay, too, because kissing happened. Love happened. Had someone (*Audrey, Audrey, Audrey,* said my heart) been a mother for a brief month before she realized she couldn't do it on her own? That was okay, too. There was strength in saying you couldn't do a thing.

No one ever had to know how strong you actually were—if they did, they would surely be scared. Inside the walls, you could be as strong as you were and no one would flinch because they'd be too busy exploring their own strength, their own light. Those girls could go into the deepest woods—see there how the wall of the caboose shimmered to show an expanse of trees?—and they'd never be lost because they didn't need flashlights or breadcrumbs, they trusted their own two feet and hands and their hearts, no matter how clumsy each was.

They could go to *Jupiter* and never be lost, because Jupiter, just like Earth, was round, and no matter how far you walked across mountains and over rivers (*what kind of rivers on Jupiter?* they want to know. All the rivers: methane, lemonade, and one of your heart's true blood) you were just walking in a big circle and eventually, you'd come back around to where you started. You might not know the place, but there would be something: a scent in the air, the way the leaves rippled in the sun, the way the water soaked through the toe of your shoe. You would know something. Just circles, after all.

Here, in these four walls packed with a thousand-thousand jars, they could float. A hand could rest in a hand, sure that this connection would remain even when those hands came apart. A mouth could taste another mouth and wonder at the perfection of it. A little girl could go from dog to girl and back again and again, and know that everyone would be waiting each time she came back. How did a person walk with four legs? It was twice as easy and you could cover twice as much ground, but you'd probably be twice as tired when you at last came to rest.

What if—

No.

And the sometimes fifth girl, who was also my sister, wanted to know: *But what happens when—*

No.

Questions were for outside. Inside was for being and floating. See that river and the way it breaks through the mountain? Those four girls who were not girls drank all night. Hydrogen, oxygen, electromagnetic waves. Was that thunder? No. No.

6. Funnel Cloud

Rum was sitting outside the caboose come morning, poking a small fire with a stick. She wore her yellow nightgown, being that her clothes had been lost to last night's transformations. The rain had stopped, but the clouds were low and thick. Still, the circus played on. There were shrieks of joy or fright—as it should be, it was hard to tell them apart. Trudy and Norma were out there somewhere, while Audrey slept on. And Rum didn't look tired or sick. Her arm was unwrapped and looked healed, which I could not explain and did not try.

"It tasted like home, Lu," Rum said before I could even ask her. She withdrew her stick from the fire, got a marshmallow, and stuck the sweet back into the low flames. "It tasted like figuring out where I was supposed to be."

I still had the taste of marmalade against my tongue; still not the tang of orange, but the taste of a dry and distant world. Like figuring out where I was supposed to be. That's what it was.

When the marshmallow was perfect, Rum gave me the stick. She put another together for herself and then said, "I felt Laika go or maybe I didn't, but there was something. The press of all that gravity in that small space. They just shot her up and ..." Rum's eyes rolled to the cloudy sky. "She's up there, either dead or alive and we're ... *alive* and I think I'm home and I'm staying, Lu. I'm staying here. Dean says I can. Please say I can."

It mattered to her, that I tell her she could, but she already knew. She had granted herself the power last night, maybe even before that—the first time she had run away, from whatever she was running from. She was ready to stop.

"You can stay," I said, and her shoulders eased under the weight she thought she still carried.

"Probably just saying that because ... I mean ... what does a person do with a girl who's also a dog? Do you think that means Norma doesn't believe in me anymore?" She grinned and jabbed her marshmallow into the flames. "Dean doesn't even know, says he's still trying to figure things out, but then I suppose we all are? How's Audrey? How's your sister?"

She never asked what happened and I never said and even when Audrey joined us at the fire, dressed in clean clothes she said were from Beth, she never told us where she had been. My brain filled in all the details just like Rum's had for Laika: a small space with too much gravity.

Trudy and Norma came back to us with Dean in tow. Rum loaded each of them up with marshmallows, but Norma kept to her cotton candy, pulling tufts from the yellow, blue, and pink beehives she carried like a bouquet. Her eyes rested briefly on Rum, then flicked away, and while I hoped Rum hadn't seen, the brief downturn of her mouth said she had.

"Suppose you're going to want a ride home," Audrey said to me as she tossed her marshmallow stick into the fire.

I looked at the faces around the fire: Rum and Trudy and Norma, and though this was only Sunday, they were not the faces that had looked back at me on Friday. These were not the girls who would rather climb into the back of the Rambler and ride home safely. I thought of the body spread in the water, of the strange birds above us, the dog in the dark. Did Trudy and

Norma know that Rum was staying? That she had found her home?

I reached for Audrey's hand. "Not due 'till dinner," I said. "We'll be late, but we can get there, unless you want company."

Audrey's fingers closed warm around mine and I felt the way she was shaking. Way down inside where no one would ever know. "I think I can get there," she said, soft as the clouds of cotton candy Norma inhaled.

Before, I wouldn't have cared, my sister leaving us to head off on her own, but when she did now, it was a strange thing. Was it strange for the moon to always rise opposite the sun, to skirt through its shadow and then away again? It was only natural, what the sky did day in and out.

Leaving Rum was something entirely different. It was us leaving her in this strange place with its giants and dwarfs and dog-men and angels. I didn't want to go, not until she held my hands and told me that sometimes, you just have to launch yourself into space. Sometimes you come back down and sometimes you don't, and either is okay. Gravity was a thing, sometimes with us and sometimes not and fighting it was stupid, and it was that thought I held to as we left the circus and Rum and Dean and Beth and were swallowed up once more by the Philadelphia streets.

It was a quiet journey with quiet company. Outside the circus, Norma drew back into herself and Trudy kept her distance, too, and we crossed all the things we had already crossed: the woods, the bridge and its river now empty of its dead body, and the woods once more, and then slowly to home. Norma and Trudy split in different directions, Norma with Trudy's transistor radio in hand, Trudy's pompadour bouncing into the dusk as if untouched by all gravity.

And me, coming home to our white house that stood so tall and seemed so alien in the darkening night. I found Joel and

Audrey on the porch and slowed my steps so as not to interrupt, but it was Audrey who drew her hands from Joel's clumsy grasp and shook her head, interrupting whatever apologies he had been making.

I was walking up the drive as he was walking down and he blanched to see me. I offered him a smile that was just too cocky and angry, the memory of bleeding Audrey in my arms far too fresh. He should have been there, but should haves didn't do anyone a lick of good.

"Sometimes you just have to launch yourself into space, Joel."

I brushed past him, stepping into the house where my parents were hollering because I was late and what, had I run away with the circus? Been eaten by a wolf? Audrey needed to explain why she came home without me and surely only a wolf would have complicated the simple journey to the circus.

But that wasn't the story I was interested in hearing. The story I found myself gravitating toward as I joined the shouted conversation and assured them I wasn't, in fact, Little Lucy Hood, was a story that involved a girl who traveled to Mars and Jupiter and beyond without ever leaving Earth. The story of a girl who learned how to shine without anyone ever looking at her, shining simply because she did what she loved. She turned ordinary things into extraordinary things, and sent ships named *Viking* and *Pioneer* plunging into the solar system.

This girl studied the mountains of Mars and deconstructed the clouds of Jupiter, and fell in love with a tiny, tiny rock that she called Hannah Fisher and no one ever knew why and that was all right, because she knew. Sometimes gravity was with us and sometimes it wasn't, but either way—I had to launch myself into space.

EBB STUNG BY THE FLOW

1940, THE TRANS-SIBERIAN RAILWAY

We are a train, tonight comprised of eighteen cars. Our shape and size are dictated by the needs of Jackson's Unreal Circus and Mobile Marmalade. Sometimes we are smaller, and sometimes we stretch long. Inside, cars can expand for miles, with golden savanna, gray tundra, wildflower meadow; inside, cars can be but a thin metal frame around towering chalk cliffs. Outside, seawater rushes in our wake, and sometimes, arctic snow.

Tonight, because the circus dictates, we dare wander into a world on the edge of war. We skim over slipstream Russian rails by moonlight, ghosting before another train running heavy with war machines. We draw back, allowing the other to surge ahead; if we are lightning, they are thunder. We send a plume of steam into the oily night-dark skies, a low whistle vibrating through metal and wood and back again. The other train has no consciousness nor do I expect one; there is only the rumble of metal and the spit of fire in response to my call. Filthy men feed its coal-black engines; it thrums onward, through the ghost of us.

What remains of the body I was is but a severed hand resting within the steam engine, with a golden cross folded into the palm. I was sworn to Christ as Sister Jerome Grace, but I was always more than that. I was she who wove the people of the world into consciousness and being, she who spun every thread into existence and divided them into singular lives. I was she who sent the immeasurable threads through my sisters' hands, so they could measure, and in turn, sever.

We do this still—the train goes where I will it, and we are drawn where the world needs us. We are life, we are death; we are that which stands between. We allowed ourselves to be carried away, allowed ourselves to love, to die, and become a train that circles the world entire as the circus dictates. We are four hundred, eighty-five tons of glorious metal and wood, our engine wheels paired four, six, six, and four, and there is *nowhere* we have not been. Nowhen. My sister Lisbeth keeps the jars, fragments of time into which we may slip. My sister Mae measures every second and every breath, and through her, I feel the weight of the artillery shell as the breech locks around it. I taste the metal tang that coats Mae's tongue; she knows the fragmentary shrapnel vibrating beneath the shell's sleek metal jacket.

It is nothing I can stop and I cannot warn the other train; there is only scorching, speeding metal. I cannot speak to the workers; they have no affinity for such things. The few passengers, the façade of the train's true intent, are also beyond my reach, though I can feel them within the train's speeding cars, most heavy with sleep. They will not be able to flee; Lisbeth's hands will cut all night.

The weight of the shell in the air is monstrous as it vaults from its barrel and into the night. Only eight pounds—Jackson was bigger when I pulled him from the daffodil box on the foundling hospital's steps. I count the rounds as they fly from the barrels—four, six, six, two, and empty. A breath. Between the realization that they will fire, they have already launched, destruction approaching at five hundred, seventy-one feet per second.

The train in front of us bucks off the tracks, the engine rearing like a spooked horse. The tender whips free from its coupler when the car behind it explodes, star-bright against the night like the entire world has gone up. The tender, full of coal and water, pancakes into the engine, and shrapnel falls like rain, shell and train shattering outward through the night.

We cannot avoid the wreck. They carry three hundred tons of war machines, and they cannot stop.

The fire blossoms inferno bright, the heat yanking me from the slipstream rails. We fist through the other train, through war machines and soldiers and the civilians they meant to hide behind; through rubber melting against metal and into flesh. I believe for one breath that we will make it—that I can guide us free and clear, thread through a flaming needle, and who better with thread than she who spun every thread into conscious actuality? But the explosion has thrown us into the war-torn reality I had hoped to avoid. Jackson wanted only to play along these tracks, and now one train is inside the other; my body inside that of the smoldering train, hand submerged in melting glove.

I reach. The needs of the circus dictate above all else that we do *not* die, we do not succumb to such mortal destruction, but in this moment it is beyond me, and my cars emerge wholly into this reality, blowing the other train wide open, as we in turn are blown. Fire, ballooning against my back.

We are blown, and I am falling from a great height, a height that is incomprehensible, for I am a train upon tarnished, well-run tracks. But I am falling through the air itself. I feel the air on cheeks and between fingers and it is autumn that fills my senses, *autumn*, and I've not smelled anything but coal in so long. I blink and cough, soot coating my tongue. Trains do not have tongues.

I stare at the ruin of a train above me, what was once a roof now blown open, metal peeled back the way one might open an orange. Beyond the metal maw, trees. So many trees, their leaves fluttering gold so that for a moment, I think the sky is made of leaves. But beyond the gold, the blue sky of morning. A cool nose presses against my cheek.

Cold, wet, and a puff of breath that is warm, before a warmer tongue licks me. The sensation is so extraordinary, I shriek and pedal backwards through the debris of the train car. I regard the monkey before me. Soot-coated Ichabod stares, as startled as I am, his chest rising and falling with each vexed breath.

Unbroken, I sit up, but my consciousness that once inhabited the train now inhabits another body. A body of breath and blood, a body I helped raise from youth into adulthood. Jackson's hands have become my own, gnarled and aching. I should be broken, thrown as I was through the wreckage, but it is only the hands that hurt, each finger having been broken years before.

Ichabod chitters as he climbs into my arms, sits on my shoulder. It is a curious thing to have a shoulder large enough for an animal to rest upon. Ichabod's tail curls around my neck, the end tickling my chin. I laugh, and the sound startles both of us, bright in the wreck of the train.

I stand on uncertain legs. The memory of skirts swirls through me, strange and new to me and the consciousness that still inhabits this body.

"Jackson?" I ask.

The train groans, metal shifting, as elsewhere in the wreckage other circus animals and performers emerge from our near-doom. Inside me, it feels as if there is someone else moving around, someone who is as surprised as I am that I now inhabit his body. I take a breath and I want to cry at the sensation of lungs expanding. I marvel at the scents of burning oil and spilled blood and crushed trees, and turn in a slow circle, mindful of the debris that blocks my steps but walking even so. I relish the feel of every sharp angle underfoot; the way a piece of glass shatters beneath my weight, the slip of dust beneath the sole of my boot.

Jackson does not prevent me from moving, not even as I touch his body. I place a cautious hand atop my head and it is Jackson's own, full of thick, dark hair. My hands pat down chest, belly, groin, and when I linger to study the way a body curves and responds to touch, I am satisfied that Jackson *cannot* stop me. This body has become my own, and the world spreads out before me in ways it has not in so long. I can step off the rails, I can walk with feet and touch with hands.

Within the crumpled doorframe of the train car, my sister Lisbeth appears. Her brown skin is streaked with blacker soot, and blood darkens the hem of her dress. I can feel her heartbeat; her wound is deep, and even though it will heal—we were not made for dying—worry spikes through me. It's fear that brightens Lisbeth's eyes; she knows it is not Jackson who stands before her, can sense me within his body.

I scatter from the wreckage of the two trains, me inside Jackson. We move through warm darknesses until at the end of a long corridor, we see a familiar twelve-paned window within the foundling hospital. Once, long ago, it was part of a shrine to Mary, and candlewax clings to the marble sill. Our hands don't hurt; we are small, and young, and this was almost the beginning.

Jackson's face peers back at me from the lowest window-pane, and though I still feel his consciousness inside, it's only me who moves the body, and we run. We have not run with feet and legs for years, and the sensation of pumping heart and lungs is thrilling; we run to our room where we collapse onto the thin-mattressed bed and we do not care about the spring that pokes us; every awareness is glory.

The room is smaller than we remember, a narrow shelf above the bed holding that old daffodil box, which is now crammed full of penny dreadfuls. I cannot help but reach up for them, pulling the box down against my chest the way one might a newborn. The books are not dusty; they are well-read and well-loved, and I press my nose into the spread pages the way one might press into a spread woman; I inhale, instantly intoxicated. Each endpaper is marked with Jackson's careful script, his name written in a careful hand. But there is a book missing from the collection, taken from him, and this sends a spike of anger through me.

Memory propels me back to the corridor. Within Jackson's young body, the true nature of him tries to slither free. He does not want to admit to this form, has not yet willingly become it. I could force him into it, could open the space and allow this body to give way, but I don't. Arms and legs and heart and lungs are precious to me, so long having been made of wheels and axles and metal; I revel in the power of flesh as we burst through Timothy's door, to find him sprawled on his bed.

"Where are they?" we demand.

"W-what—"

It takes no strength at all to lift him from the bed. There is a strange satisfaction in the way he tumbles to the floor between wall and bed, the way he cowers and watches us over the edge of the mattress. We rip the blankets and pillows from the bed; we pull the drawers from the side table. It only briefly registers that Timothy owns even less than we do—that what he treasures most seem to be jacks and a rotted rubber ball. And still, we find the books, pressed between mattress and iron headboard. They have been there so long the metal headboard has made an indentation upon the wood-pulp covers.

We leave the books there, our hands coming back to the boy. We haul him up with a strength we should not possess, and the power in my hands is astonishing. We pull this boy out from the gap between bed and wall and down the hall, where he only whimpers, still trying to convince himself he is within a nightmare and not the real world.

The foundling hospital was a strange place after all, and boys always went missing. These were, of course, those children who would not be missed, for no one outside these walls knew they existed. Boys always went missing, and soon others came to take their place.

Timothy had tried, in days prior, to befriend Jackson with candies and fresh socks and though Jackson had allowed this boy into his space, he had quickly discerned the boy's actual target: the penny dreadfuls. It had been easy to turn the boy's eagerness back on himself, for everyone wanted something. Jackson lured the boy into a deeper friendship, requesting more of his time, more of his attention, until the boy had only Jackson to turn to when something went wrong. Inevitably, something did go wrong; Jackson ensured it did. *I* ensured it did?

For here we were, stepping into a room that should not exist, tangling the boy into what appeared to be cobwebs but became ropes, but became Jackson's arms as his true self slithered beyond even what control I maintained over the body. He held a danger none could entirely understand—not even me who made him into a great titan whose proud head brushed the stars. His boundless winged body was that of a man down to his belly, but from there, he was all viper coils, his strong hands reaching east and west as far as he desired. A fearful dragon with a dark tongue and darker fires.

Folly made him thus. *My* folly. Revulsion is a new sensation, my mouth sharp with vomit, when I see what we have done to Timothy. Jackson should never have been bound into flesh, but he wanted to know what it was to be a human body, wanted to know every aspect. Who was I to say no. I am she who creates, not she who cuts and denies.

In the darkness, Lisbeth's scissors blaze and I flee.

Night severs itself from day, to reveal me and my sisters, bloody in bright snow. We pick ourselves from the ground, naked and steaming, never children but newborn nonetheless. I unfold like a flower, petals seeking unseen sun. There is light without warmth, the air a still limbo around us. I reside still within Jackson's body as I look upon my sisters; I am not sure if they can see me for me as the threads slick down my thighs and into their hands. Mae holds the threads' weight constantly, bearing that which we cannot; Lisbeth's hands are sharp, sending to ruin what Mae deems done.

Above us, the skeleton of a dying temple, its cracked ceiling flaking with blue paint that once cradled golden stars. The threads spilling from my body surge up the columns, wrapping them until the threads basketweave themselves into a stained and ancient fabric, into a rippling circus tent where the strongman stands in the thick shadows. He reeks of bile soap, the tang of slaughtered animals never quite extinguished. He smells like Lisbeth; like ever-present death. Is he my guide? Isn't there always a guide?

"Probably wouldn't help if you talked." The voice in my throat is startling; the feel of tongue against teeth and palate.

Jackson does not smoke, but I draw a pack of cigarettes from his shirt pocket. I tap it against my thigh and try to unwrap the cellophane. Jackson's misshapen fingers are no longer meant for such detail work. I cannot grasp the seam at the pack's end no matter how I try. The strongman only watches; his hands not meant for such finery either.

Jackson wears a knife at his side and it comes out of its leather sheath easily enough; its hilt is thick, grasped by even these crumpled hands. Its point is razor sharp and moves through the cellophane as if through air. The cellophane curls as it parts, like a body coming undone. I hitch the blade under the gleaming wrap and pull. It crinkles as I slide the knife away and I tap the pack again.

I thumb the lid up and one cigarette slides smoothly out. I haven't smoked in years—haven't breathed in years. The cigarette feels nice between my lips, solid, and it smells grand, something to hold onto in the gloom of the train car—No. Not the train, but the circus tent wavers around us and my worry takes hold of me; worry that I will flee this space before I understand it.

The strongman never speaks. He only stares from sunken eyes that show me my own reflection. I am Jackson, with misshapen hands and bent body. No matter how Jackson may present himself to the rest of the world—businessman, showman—he is ever this huddled mass. And I within him, to undo what I did?

Can I control where I might go? This body wants to dance. Wants to kiss a willing mouth. Wants to drink water and be drunk in return. I do not want to stand before the strongman and—be judged in silence.

I draw a slow breath and move to the strongman's side, this

man who does not move or speak, but simply is. When I move toward him, so too does the circus tent move; fabric melts into metal and the wreck of the trains rises around us. The strongman's stare becomes the weight of the world upon me; if he is judge, this is his evidence. I have broken something.

I step out of the train, boots crunching over the stones cluttering the shoulder of the tracks. Wreckage is thrown everywhere—how very careless someone has been with this train. I pinch the cigarette between my fingers. Paper crinkles, tobacco rains.

I try to pick familiar shapes from the wreckage and see too many I know. The Ferris wheel arcs dark against the clouded sky, its gondolas scattered. A carousel horse is frozen in midleap, a bear smashed on the tracks beneath it. Tent fabric drapes trees and bodies. The dead litter everywhere, and it isn't only friends but people from the other train. Soldiers melted to their war machines. They have been transformed by fire, the violence smoothed from every sharp line.

And I think, if I had not been the train, had not been severed from my body, had not bound Jackson into mortal flesh, this would not have come to pass. Could I have prevented it? It is not enough to flicker backward with Lisbeth's jars of preserved time; it is not enough to return to those hospital walls, or the bloody snow field—there is something else. Something that needs doing? Something that needs.

The scent of marmalade hangs in the strange air, and then it is raining marmalade from the trees. Globules of orange and gold patter upon the gray stones, the gleaming rails. Marmalade sizzles as it strikes the train engine, as if she were still warm and breathing but when I slide my hand over the metal, it is cold and empty. The low thrum that once filled the metal husk is gone. Within the belly of the engine, the hand clasping the golden cross remains, blackened and charred by fire, splattered with lemon marmalade.

I close my hands tight despite the pain; I crush the cigarette to dust and bow my head. I do not know what is being asked of me. I will myself away from the wreck, trying to remember what it was to have a body of flesh, a body that had needs and wants. Simple things: air, water, clothes when the world grows cold. Complicated things: touch, communion, the desire to be full of all things, always.

When my severed hand was placed in the hot belly of the speeding dragon—Jackson thought it so, the first time he saw the train on the rails in the rain—I was named anew. Reborn into a machine that would cross the world, would cross time, going where and when she would, carrying those beloved far beyond the existence of their fated threads.

When you give a thing a name, you give it power. I was given an extraordinary name and thus, an extraordinary power. I push away, past. I reach for everything. I root the body in the world it would have known. The world comes into focus like a stuttering filmstrip, black and white and then on fire with neon and gaslight. Popcorn and cotton candy pervade the air and dragging in a breath leaves me dizzy; somewhere, blood has been spilled, because its fetid layer lingers under everything, keeping everyone warm, filled.

I pay no attention to the reflection of my body in the misshapen mirrors I pass. I am light and unbroken, and even spreading my hands brings no pain. I reach for everything I want. I have never been allowed to want, so I allow the world to flood me.

I caress crones and angels alike; I dance with satyrs and share potions with a man in a black mask that shows me my own face—*my* face, writhing threads that refuse to be knit into any one feature. The potion steals my breath; the man drinks it down as if it is his own and grows into a huge dragon against the night sky; wings of stars and nebulous breath, and he's gone, screaming in fire and longing.

This circus fills my veins, delights like the traveling circus never did. We were freaks; homeless and wandering for eternity. Broken from the world, a fragment of glass pressed into a bleeding heel. *This* circus is life, rooted and fixed into the spine of creation.

The lights drain from the world when I turn a corner; the calliope music grows distant and now there is only the scent of blood and tears. Sweet treats do not exist in these dark lanes. Within the cages that stack the alleys, small black girls have been dressed like daisies, their delicate petals splattered with blood. They are two-headed and three-legged and all watch me pass with silent, black eyes. Even smaller girls reside in jars, their lids spun tight, gifted with single air-holes. Farther on, girls have been crafted into strange and terrible things; bats, cats, rats. It is a broken poem, one that ends in the hideous display of what I know to be a siren; this beautiful creature is part woman, part bird, but here she is only all misery. She is pinned to a board, oil-slick feathers streaked with saliva, blood, ejaculate.

"Agnessa?"

She lifts her head, her familiar gaze defiant. I am struck as if by a fist, straight in my throat, and I run, refusing this nightmare. But I cannot go back, for the lanes have closed themselves away. I go forward into the unending labyrinth that leads me to him.

Of course it's him. Jackson, on display as he might have always been had it not been for *me*. Jackson was only ever a misunderstood horror. No longer did he possess any human aspect but was wholly as he had first been made: thick scaled body, slavering fanged mouth, countless tentacles snapping as he tries to escape the cage holding him. He is nearly the color of blood, suffused with fury as every attempt to pry the cage apart fails. He takes no notice of me, which allows me to get to the very edge of the cage before he greets me with violence. One tentacle coils around my throat and shoulders, effortlessly lifting me from the ground.

"I know your face," he snarls.

His touch gentles, and in my pulse I can hear the click-clack of a train over metal tracks. It never happened here because I, because *we* never crossed threads. After his creation, we never saw each other again; he never asked me to bind him into a mortal body, and the world has fallen to ruin. I see the scars that mark his body, the evidence of humiliations which must be meager compared to those he has known on the inside. In this place where he cannot even see the sky.

I have no sisters here, no sisters who might help me undo what has been done. In my terror, I reach for them. Across the years and unreal construct of this place—*this* place never happened, I tell myself. I tell *Jackson*. In concert we shriek as the world is undone, bodies flayed in a ceaseless, consuming wind. Within its heart, my sister Mae who bears all things; who waits, who holds even my thread and might end this torment.

Jackson's sleeping compartment is no more lavish than any other on the train, though it is possessed of a single curtain drawn across its entire width for a measure of privacy beyond that which the locked car door provides. Against this black cotton curtain, Mae's naked body glows and I linger to see her back, am drawn by her breath.

With Jackson's ruined fingers I pull the burned marmalade spatters from my sister's skin, from the long line of her neck. She is not burned, though her skin flushes pink every time I peel away another piece of candied marmalade. As I go, her skin smooths back to its ivory, the color of elephant tusk, the color of a dream turned inside out, and there is as always that low sheen, that shimmer that tells me to dip my fingers in and watch the ripples. I stroke a finger down Mae's arm, starting at the crest of her shoulder, lingering in the concave curve of her elbow. Her pulse thrums hello.

In the gloom that falls between us, I cannot tell the marmalade's flavor until my tongue is on it. Burnt limes. My mouth works the splatter with a strange fervor; teeth and tongue glance Mae's skin, lightly marking her, and that is when I feel the slide of her hand into my hair. I expect Mae to pull me away, for it rests with her to say when a thing is finished, but Mae's hold only tightens. Does she know it's me, her sister within Jackson's body? I exhale, teeth closing on flesh and not marmalade, and the low sound that fills the curtained space comes from us both.

The press of tongue becomes too much for the skin to endure. The skin that anchors Mae in this world parts, dissolves, and I fall into the reality of her. More coils of thread; familiar spools and spindles. I look for my own path; each of us must also have a thread. But I never find it, and understand that I never will (that I cannot, for some things are forbidden even to us). I look until it's Mae's mouth I find—*I want to kiss a willing mouth*—and I'm kissing her, and she's kissing me, and she knows me for her sister, for the beginning of all things.

As if she can sense my questions, she licks them from my mouth, carries them away, and for the moment, there is only the blessed tide of her body rushing over mine. No gentle swell but a wave to knock me to my knees. Mae lifts Jackson's ruined hands, and in her eyes they are whole again, unbroken, and if not beautiful then usable. I slide them over breast and belly, fitting fingers into Mae one by one by one, until she breaks.

"This isn't the end," Mae says.

She strokes her fingers down the inside of my arm. My skin

peels back under the gentle pressure. No muscle, no bone, only the threads wriggling like fish beneath a calm pool, blue until Mae touches them. Her finger is electric inside me. Her fingers plait me into sections for study, for love, for disposal—but the disposal never comes. I ache for it and it never comes.

"Everything ends," I whisper and the hot, broken metal of the train groans as cold rain pours from the sky.

"Not everything."

After the rain, fog swallows the world. I emerge from the wreck of the train, into a cottony wall of fog that obscures everything but vague tree limbs above. A skeletal dog trots out of the fog; she's following the line of the tracks, ignoring the hulk of the train, but draws to a stop when she sees me. Long legged and lean like she hasn't eaten in—

"Years," I whisper, and my voice sounds large in the dense air. The dog's ears go up, like small bits of fabric in a sudden breeze. They gleam with wetness; she has been walking in the rain, this dog the color of fog. Everything is familiar.

The dog pads closer, then sinks onto her haunches, watching. Her eyes reflect a shrunken world, though when she blinks, the landscape shifts, vanishes, then slowly returns. I watch her until she yawns, and then I head down the track, along the burned length of trains. The dog follows me as I poke through the rubble.

The survivors do not see me, and when I find Jackson's body in the rubble, I understand why. Yet, I still occupy this body; the hands I reach with are still his own, if under my control. His body is flattened beside the tracks, his cheek clammy beneath my fingers. Jackson is dead, the train is demolished, and I— Could go anywhere.

This is the choice. It is mine to say, when never it was before—though I am still the point of creation. This: the moment before.

I lift a burned scrap of paper from the ground, a fragment of a poster, and the dog sidles closer. She stretches her neck to take a breath of air around the burned poster and I, moving slow, set the paper before her. She bends her head and the paper sticks to her nose. I pluck it free and fold it into my hand.

"Walk farther down with me," I say. The fog keeps my voice close, and the dog's ears perk. She watches when I gesture toward the caboose that seems to have turned itself inside out.

The caboose's contents litter the world. Jars of marmalade exploded under the intense heat, splatters of sweet having adhered themselves to the train, the tracks, the ground. Burned droplets of sugar and fruit drip from the meager canopy of trees. Oil-slick colors have melted into stained glass mockeries the dog licks.

I find one of Lisbeth's cooking knives in the debris, under a flood of orange marmalade which is burned to an amber lozenge. One of her mixing bowls rests on its side, clouded dreams spilling onto the railroad ties; the stars are black now, the mass no longer churning out the star stuff that makes everything and everyone. A bell jar sits where the caboose's back door used to be, a miniature Ferris wheel captured under its perfect dome. There isn't a fingerprint on it, nor dust, and even when the fog reaches down, the wheel recoils from the glass. Untouchable.

A marmalade jar rests against a railroad tie, whole and uncracked. I roll the time-heavy jar into my hand, and before me stand my sisters—Mae and Lisbeth—and the ground is wet with rain and blood both. The sun is out and it is snowing and I push myself to standing. I offer Lisbeth the knife, Mae the jar. We could leave this place at long last, we three; we could allow the train to keep this broken fate, or we could choose one better. But to take this path, we must be bound as we were.

This is the decision.

Cold fog, the whine of a dog (the whine of a *god*), and the press of a willing mouth against my own.

We are a train, tonight comprised of forty-seven cars. Our shape and size are dictated by the needs of Jackson's Unreal Circus and Mobile Marmalade. Sometimes we are smaller, and sometimes we stretch long—as long as we ever have, tonight! We run slipstream rails alone under moonlight—it's cold here, but growing warmer, sunrise on the horizon. Within us, cars expand for miles as needed: green with dense jungle, polka-dotted with blue-eyed lakes, deserts tonguing thorned acacia trees. Sometimes, glittering snow rushes in our wake; sometimes, warm seawater, gushing from hidden springs.

I was a body.

I am, once more, a train.

LADY MARMALADE

1946, YOUR HOMETOWN

"My old San Francisco, Beth?"

The lime rind is slick between her brown fingers and she looks up to Jackson's face, which peers through the caboose's side window. Weathered, lined, still the color of a baby's belly in the gloom of pre-dawn.

Beth is not her name, though she responds well enough to it by now. Perhaps one of the countless jars that line the wall of the caboose-turned-bakery contains her real name, but if so, it is pushed well to the back, gathering dust, cobwebs, forgetfulness. She has not forgotten; she cannot.

She flicks the rind into the bowl before her, wipes fragrant fingers over her apron, and stands from her stool. She has time to go. Fingers trace over soda-lime glass, milk glass; amber, cobalt, green. Ball blue, violet, clear, and black. Jewel tone marmalades press against the curves: lime, lemon, orange, quince, pomegranate. Colorless fogs, rivers, rains, and bogs. Sparrow hearts. A first blush, a last breath, countless in betweens. Her fingers close around a square jar. She gathers one more, this one empty, before leaving the caboose. Eamonn the dwarf perches on the counter, hovers over the rind bowl, and does not look at the bell jar which sits on a shelf at his eye level. Inside, a Ferris wheel stands beside a tree caught in perpetual autumn.

"Just a little jaunt," Jackson says and slips his arm through hers before she takes the lid off the first jar and they vanish as though never there.

Jackson is a jar himself, containing in every aspect the time he wishes to visit. Beth dips her hand into him and the streets permeate her skin. Stone cobbles run like gooseflesh and bridges arc where her fingers once did, stretching into piers, looping backward into avenues soaked with smoke, shade, spice. Through Jackson she can smell the salty ocean the iron rails, the stink of love and bloom of despair. She walks, her feet inside his shoes, her fingers around the knob of the red-flecked door he opens. His slim sketchbook is hidden in a woman's wrapper pocket. Beth feels the trespass of his fingers into the pocket, the tug of a thread as the sketchbook slips out of time's place.

Jackson whispers, "Four years later, this place is gone."

Time does not matter to Beth, but it is a thing which anchors Jackson and others like him. These rooms haunt him; he hates and loves them by turn. What becomes of them in four years? Part of her wants to know. Part of her presses hands against that pane of glass and peers. Still, she can't reach it, not even through Jackson; for he won't be there to remember it by sight or smell. She wishes time did matter, would wish it with all her heart if she still possessed such a thing. She slides the empty jar into his hand and hears the whisper of the book curling inside glass.

"And, back."

Eamonn is still not looking at the bell jar when they return in a blink, steaming in the summer air, the opalescent light. It is not heat that sluices from them, but chill, for it was winter Jackson wanted, claiming his book from a lady he refuses to name. Beth doesn't ask; she never does.

Jackson takes his leave with his jar. Beth slides her jar against another—Exposition Universelle, where Jackson admired the gauge railway—then settles into the well-worn groove her bottom has made upon her stool. She returns to the lime rind, cutting, cutting. Eamonn perches—not looking—until at last he turns away and moves for the dough bowl. He peels back the damp tea towel. The scent of yeast fills the caboose.

The carnival opens as the sun touches the tips of the long field grass, to allow the crowds to capitalize on the warm yeast rolls, the glazed buns, the sour breads. Eamonn's large hands cradle each one as they come free from their pans, then set them to cool along the caboose windowsills. His slippered feet leave small impressions in the flour scattered over the counter. The tails of his black and green striped coat sweep up after him.

Beth hears the soft murmurs from several paces away; older ladies dressed in their Sunday best though it may be Wednesday or later. Older ladies clutching straw pocketbooks (adorned with flowers made of gleaming plastic jewels) with gloved hands, every step tentative though not because of age. They fear the very thing that draws them forward.

"It smells like my childhood."

"Mine, too. Do you think they have—Ah! Elephant ears!"

A thin arm points toward the banners which snap in the warm breeze above the caboose, while the scent of fresh fried dough reaches the woman's nose. She closes her eyes a moment and stands in place, near a swoon.

Eamonn extracts the fried dough while Beth readies the marmalade. Lemon and a touch of twenty-two, Beth knows, and has the confection ready as the women come to the window. She lets Eamonn deal with them; they love to fuss over his fancy coat and marvel at how small he is. He either doesn't hear them or doesn't mind, for he is never put-out when they laugh.

The lemon elephant ear seems to melt against the woman's tongue; Beth can almost feel it upon her own. It tastes like the woman's childhood, but the marmalade brings with it another memory, the memory of a younger body that once balanced on a high wire. *Maybe an umbrella, Miss Sophie,* a dark-haired boy says. His eyes rake up her stockinged leg and she loses her balance, plummeting.

"Oh." It arrives as a soft exhale. "Do you—Do you sell this lemon marmalade?"

Of course they do and Beth reaches into the long line of bright jars, retrieving the proper one for Miss Sophie. A square of fabric that looks to have been cut from a circus tent just that morning covers the lid. Beth ties it with a yellow ribbon that makes Miss Sophie recall the feel of that young man's tie between her fingers.

Beth feels nothing as they walk away and she turns back to the jars which line the west wall. The shelves which Rabi made her are worn with time and fingerprints, allowing only one gap for the thin window on that side. Every jar is different and Beth knows where each came from the way she knows the lines on her palm. Her fingers dance over them now, glass shoulders and corked tops; embossed lettering, the thick curve of a sealed lip. Sunlight sneaks through the windows to fragment itself in the bottom of the jars. This shattered sunlight scatters across the shelves which bracket the back door, over the counter and sweltering stoves, across Beth's brown cheeks in a stained glass mosaic. Small black monkey feet scamper across the topmost shelf as Ichabod steals inside, leaping down to Eamonn's shoulder where he chatters at the customers.

"Pomegranate pear?"

The voice at the window draws her attention. The young man there is tall, for his eyes meet Beth's over the sill. His eyes are the color of the bottle just above the window, its label a scrawl that only Beth knows: *Co. Kerry, morning mist, November.*

Pomegranate pear was a flavor she didn't want to make, but she still did, turning the golden pears into a smooth chocolate-brown butter, dribbling in the crimson seeds. Beth had allowed herself one spoonful before jarring it, admitting to herself it was one of her best. She reaches for the jar now, fingers knowing where it rests, but her fingers close around nothingness.

Amid the cluster of jars upon the counter, there is a vacant space, a jar-shaped space, a space pomegranate pear should occupy but doesn't. She looks past the marmalades, beyond the canisters and knotgrass, the jarred yeast and dormouse footprints. The deep opal bowl which houses dreams is still near to overflowing and she drapes a soft towel across it before she moves to the bell jar, fingers printing the lid before she works up and up, past jarred breaths and bottled cities; past boxed fields and ribbon-bound supernumerary rainbows. No pomegranate pear and when she comes back to the window; no young man.

It is easier to move a single person than it is the entire train and its company. Beth can and does move the train when necessary, even enjoys the challenge, but takes a different kind of pleasure when it's just one person; when it's just herself.

She opens the jar to find herself on a Himalayan plain, in a time before humanity has discovered this place. The air here is cold, pinks her cheeks. She picks her way toward the pomegranate trees which line the foothills and opens a wide-mouth jar. Two pomegranates will fit inside, little else. She twists the lid into place then sinks into the dark soil at the base of the trees. If she keeps still, the sunlight sinks through her and she hears only the wind.

She doesn't keep still. She hears the faint beat of a heart and pushes up from the soil. It cannot be her own, she refuses the very idea, but then she sees the shadowed figure on the hill before her. The heartbeat lurches.

She runs. Clutching jars against her sides, she runs toward the figure that shouldn't be here. Shouldn't be here and she screams. He's not supposed to be in this place—she broke all the jars he ever had claim to, removing those places and years from her reach. (*But you didn't, oh you didn't*, whispers a distant voice.) Still, he leaps into motion, long legs and flailing arms and that shock of curling black hair. She knows the color of his eyes even if she cannot see them now.

He evades her advance. The pomegranates jostle in their jar, making a solid thumping rhythm against her ribs. The empty jar in her other hand slips and she tightens her hold. Don't drop it, she tells herself. *Don't. Don't be stuck here with this shadow-creature.* Her feet come down hard with every stride.

"Don't. Don't. Don't."

The word comes with every fall of her right foot. And then: "Don't go."

But he goes; vanishes through another stand of pomegranate trees as a breath of wind, pulling her after, turning her heel over head until she does not know which way is up. If the ground is blue, then so be it. She feels as though something precious has been taken from her yet again, even though it was lifetimes ago. Once, she could have counted the time on her fingers, but not now. Even so, she remembers the feeling; it remains a broken place that never healed straight. Staggering, she turns from the trees and runs.

She reaches for the train, pulling caboose walls tall around her, patching in every jar she knows by touch in the dark. She pictures the rusting Ferris wheel under the gleam of the glass and the sugar bowl with its chipped edge and paired dormice curled inside; she draws the taste of sour dough into her mouth, swallows it down, and lets it consume her. Himalayan air slides down her arms, summer sunlight taking its place. Eamonn and Ichabod come into slow focus and she allows the jars to slip from her fingers. Eamonn startles, then moves to the broom.

She doesn't think she will ever grow tired of the sounds of the carnival. When night comes and the jars fall to darkness in their nooks, Beth closes her eyes and listens.

Even from a distance she names the lions by the sound of their voices. If the train stays in one place long enough, she comes to know the voices of the children who frequent the rides in the same way. The tightropes creak under Pasha's feet, while the cotton candy machine buzzes like an angry bee and the filaments in the electric lights hum higher and brighter. A soft moan runs below it all, something old and fluid like a river and Beth's toes curl inside her shoes, as though she were dipped in up to her ankles. The heart of the circus, dark and wet and cold and pounding.

"Miss?"

The boy standing outside the caboose is lit by the clear glass bulbs, his hair like spun gold curling into his open collar. It's warm enough that's he's barefoot and clutching two dollars in his shaking hands. Beth leans across the counter and holds to the feeling of that ancient sound at the base of all she knows. Eamonn leans, too, against Beth's shoulder as he looks out at the boy.

"My ma said—" He swallows hard, thin throat working as if he has an apple lodged there. His eyes skip to the dwarf, then back to Beth. "She said you have jams, or jellies, or summat?" He offers the money up, the bills trembling.

Beth reaches for a crate. "Did you want to spend the whole two dollars?"

She already knows he does; his mother is a bright star in his head, fully formed in a white dress splattered with blue flowers. Twelve buttons run between her breasts, from waist to throat where her own spun gold hair tangles in a knot. At present she is screaming and laughing to be let off the Ferris wheel. This woman tasted the marmalade before—three years ago?—and with it the memory of a boy she kissed when she was but twelve. A small peck, standing barefoot at the end of a lake-wet dock; the gangly boy fled and she never saw him again. Lakes and docks always make her wonder where he is. He's in New York, Beth could tell her; he tasted the marmalade five years ago and remembered that kiss as well. He never married.

"She said you would know, see."

"I know," Beth says.

Beth fills the small crate with six jars: two orange, two lemon, one lime, and one cherry jam. The cherry jam doesn't sell well, but the crew likes it—Manny says the lions like it especially well. Still, she knows this woman (Lila, the wind says) and knows these cherries will remind her of her husband. Though it is a small jar, Lila will savor it over the course of a month, remembering the warmth of his fingers and the way he held her hand when their golden-haired boy was born in a field of wheat. After, there was the sweet taste of cherry cola.

The boy runs back to his mother and Beth leaves the caboose, knowing Eamonn can sell the marmalade well enough without her for a bit. She seeks the main tent, where a cacophony of sound spills. Shards of light escape the tent flaps and vents; screams and laughter come in bursts like thunder. Inside the tent warmth, Beth keeps to the outer edge of planked bleachers, unseen as she steps past a young boy and girl who have found more to enjoy in each other's lips than they have in Rabi's center-ring show.

Vanquisher and vanisher, sink me down into this dirt and let me rest. Beth wants to speak the words to Rabi, but doesn't and won't ever. She knows too well how his talent weighs on his mind, how it's not such an easy task to make someone or something disappear. She has been asked to open a jar she would rather not; she has crossed that line, and will again. They are almost in the same business, she and he.

Beth disappears through the shadows, fingers trailing along the bleacher supports. Paper cups dot the landscape here, dropped from careless hands; she finds a wallet amid the soft dirt but leaves it there—perhaps its owner wishes to be someone else. Under the tent, everyone should be given that chance.

The Kerry-eyed boy is not within the tent. Beth knows this from the moment she enters, yet still she looks for him, an automatic response like a leg jerking when tapped. She finds instead Eamonn, at the end of the curving bleachers. He claims her hand and drags her from the tent, into the wash of yellow-white light outside. It's the parked caboose he pulls her toward and to the second empty space within it.

The bell jar is gone, a perfect faded circle in its place where the sun has worn around it all these immeasurable years. In its center sits a silver coin with an owl upon it.

In the beginning, darkness lay upon the face of the deep. When this darkness roused itself, it was the great lifting wings of a raven who was Mother Night. From her crawled doom, fate, sleep, and dreams. From her fingertips spilled the aether, the madness, and the ancient river's boatman. All things would come to an end, she decreed, even night herself as dawn crept over her wing's edge to spread warmth where there had been but cold.

To see that all things would be kept in their place, that all things would end, Mother Night divided fate, bestowing her daughters with tasks they might never finish. Every night, a breath would be stilled even if another came into being. Every night, a love would be confessed as another fell to ash.

Into her eldest daughter's hands, Mother Night placed the scissors to cut the thread, forgetting that fingers might also tie knots in severed lines. What was torn asunder might yet be joined again.

Beth remembers her name, even if no one uses it. She wishes that it were a lost thing moved elsewhere by Rabi's clever fingers; that years from now she might come across it in a corner (huddled and dusty and reaching for her) and say "oh yes, that." "I don't remember," would be a comfortable lie, the way carpeted with sugared rose petals.

In her name lingers the blade her mother gifted, a thing meant to cut so people might be at final rest. But this cutting takes its toll and, when confronted with the one thread she realizes she cannot cut, makes Beth search for other ways a thing might be ended. Gather it up, wrap it tight, seal it with a lid. Every jar becomes a knot in a thread, a way to stem the tide.

In the middle stands the discovery: that what is sealed away tends to leach into the ground no matter how hard one tries to control it. Water is meant to run; earth is meant to shift. Threads, if not cut, often fray on their own. Better then to control these things, parcel them out so that a thing doesn't end but somehow goes ever on. If a thing must end for one person, surely it can continue for another.

Yet here rises the absurdity: Beth wishes the thread she cannot cut would fray, but it is stronger than any one thing she knows. Stronger than he knows, too, and though his own sharp name cuts the strand once and twice and he walks away, meaning to go forever, there is yet that thread, spooling out through dark labyrinths. Wherever he walks, there is a trail in his wake, a trail she can trace no matter how she tries not to. She wishes to end it, slip it in a jar and hide it away, give it to another person so that she might at last be ended and rest, but she cannot.

She is bound as surely as everyone else is, to her own spooling thread. She cannot cut it. She has tried to tie it in knots so that she might run elsewhere, but she comes always again to the main line.

The thread makes a whisper as it goes, a soft hiss that reminds her of an egg in a pan. She breaks the jars, letting time evaporate—ending all Mother Night said should be ended— and even that becomes not enough. Not enough, for there he is, stealing through pomegranates, and there, in her own caboose, leaving a token for the bell jar.

In the end—

No, this is the part she cannot yet see.

The young redheaded woman comes to Beth on a warm afternoon, finding her behind the caboose washing the bowls that have overflowed the small inside sink. The bowls make a kind of music as they clink together, water streaming from them as Beth lifts them from the washtub to the rinse water.

"The little man said you were back here."

Beth is about to ask which little man but then realizes she means Eamonn. She straightens to peer through the back window, watching the dwarf and monkey dole out jars of marmalade to customers.

"Here I am," Beth says. She gently drops the bowl into the rinse water and dries her hands upon her apron. If the woman wanted marmalade, she would be up front, not back here.

"I heard that you might—might help me." She sweeps her jacket back to reveal the small bundle nestled against her chest. "I want to keep her, but can't."

The last two words are only a whisper. Tears spill over the girl's cheeks then, brightening her brown eyes. Beth clucks her tongue.

"Sometimes we can't have the things we most want," she says, looking at the pair of them long and hard. The baby makes a faint gurgle, seeming to nestle closer into its mother. Sometimes, Beth thought, even though we can't claim a thing, we are still haunted by it. "Wait here."

Beth gestures to the upended crate in the shadow of the caboose and when the girl sits, she steps into the train car. She takes down one jar of orange marmalade, then returns to the girl. The girl who frowns at her.

"I didn't come for your mar—"

"You will hush," Beth tells her and crouches before the pair of them. She sets the marmalade between her own knees, in the hard dirt, and looks up at the girl. "Stay quiet."

Beth slides a hand into the sling, finding warm darkness

inside. Her fingers seek out the curve of the baby's skull, smoothing over that downy hair before settling just above the nape. More warmth floods through Beth's palm. An unnamed daughter, born seven days ago.

She ties a small knot in the thread of life, before she divides the thread as neatly as she ever has. She splices this life from that, knowing that no matter what she does, there will always be this point for the mother to look back on. Beth cannot remove the memory of it entirely, so she changes it, infusing the marmalade which sits nearby. Even when given willingly, the loss of a child is no easy thing to bear, but when this young mother looks back onto the knot of the severed thread, she will remember only joy. She will remember the blue of the autumn sky that arced overhead when her child was conceived; she will recall the way the air cooled that night and how sharp the stars looked when they finally came out. With every bite, the young mother will be calmed.

Even so, she will still have to face the bottom of the jar, when the sweetness is gone and only clear glass remains. Will she break the jar or keep it and the memories it tries to hold? Will she seek the circus out in an attempt to find more? Beth can see all ends coming to fruition—she sees the young mother on an endless search for the train, the train which she never finds again; she sees her making the small jar the center of her universe, as if it might replace the child she gave away. This is the true price to be paid.

"What do I owe you?"

The young mother gets to her feet, the crate rocking gently. Beth rises beside her and presses the marmalade into her hands.

"Thirteen pears," she says.

The woman nods and walks away, sunlight gleaming on her auburn hair as she emerges from the caboose's shadow.

What of the child? Beth looks only far enough to see this

woman walking to the edge of town and the steepled church there. A young widowed man will notice the infant on his way into town, will raise her as his own. Beth could look farther, but she doesn't, leaving them all there for the time being. Sometimes, she doesn't want to see where the threads lead.

In the morning, Beth finds a bag of thirteen pears on the caboose's back porch. They are bruised and fragrant, and perfect for turning into butter (no pomegranate seeds this time, for they perished when their jar shattered, shot through with glass). This work keeps her busy the morning through, distracting her from the idea of the young man returning, even though the pear butter is meant for him. She refuses to acknowledge the way his name spills from her spoon every time she whisks it around the edge of her pot. It is not about her troubles, no, but those of every person outside these caboose walls. She can think on their miseries, if not her own.

She saved one pear for eating and slices another bit of it free, savoring the warm grit of it between her teeth and against her tongue. Ichabod, who perches where the bell jar once did, bends his head down and opens his mouth. Beth feeds him a slice and softly hums until the sunlight brightens the caboose and customers begin lining up at the window. She searches their eager faces yet finds no one she knows.

The disappointment is still sharp, even after all these years. She glances to the jars and reaches for County Kerry's morning mist. The jar always feels cold in her hand and weighs more than it should for mist. At this point, she doesn't even have to open this lid, for she knows the mist too well. She simply vanishes into it and is gone, her bare feet sinking into long wet grass, the scent of heather replacing that of cooking pears. She closes her eyes and turns west, walking.

She finds him where he always is, in the churchyard where they first met. He crouches at the base of a crumbling statue, scribbling in a book. She is surprised to see him—she always is, for this is how Memory wrote it. She was only searching for clovers when her path crossed his; she had never looked farther down her own thread, for knowing too much about one's future was a dreadful thing—didn't everyone agree?

In this moment, he is young—so young! His brow is not yet creased with lines of worry, for he has not met her. She hesitates. If he doesn't meet her, how much better off might they both be? She brushes that thought aside as she does every time.

"Fáilte."

He startles when she speaks, his laughter broken and loud in the gloom of morning. He tilts his book and she can see the image there, a church bell tower emerging from the morning's fog. She glances past the statuary to see the church herself.

"I didn't think anyone came out here," he says. He stands, setting his book on the statue's base, watching her with reserve. She is intruding into his private space, the space he has shared with no other.

"You came out here," she says. She picks her way past him, leaving footprints in the mud. She crouches beside a statue to Saint Peter and rolls her jar on the ground. It makes a faint tinkling noise, as if something other than mist is caught inside.

Later, he will think he dreamed her and Beth almost wishes she had kept it to that, but she can't. She knows she will follow him. Nothing sparks her interest the way he does; nothing will haunt her the way he will.

She sits with him all afternoon, silent while he draws. He doesn't ask anything of her, shares the orange he has brought, and when she rises to leave, makes to follow. She doesn't stop him, knowing that as she begins to pull caboose walls back around her, he will pause on the muddy track, studying the line of footprints that are once there and then gone, as though the strange girl became the mist itself.

Mist falls from her shoulders as she comes back to the train. Deliberately, she lets the jar slip from her frozen fingers; it hits the floor with a solid thud and does not shatter. Beth watches it roll away from her and then back, resting against her muddy toes. It is the second jar she cannot break.

The first jar is the bell jar.

Her younger sister offers it to her in the depth of a night so dark Beth thinks that Mother Night has returned for good. The jar is strangely warm, like a living thing though it is made of glass. Beth cannot immediately see what it contains and for that she is grateful; when she can—when dawn's first sun breaks through the glass and illuminates the wheel and tree inside— her breath sticks in her throat. She knows that this eternal autumn will be her undoing (*salvation*, that distant voice whispers), but not precisely how.

She keeps the jar with her, throughout all the years she can count. It sits at her side, upon a shelf, or buried in a chest; it is never more than a dozen steps away. In one house, she can see it from anywhere she may be, like a bright pinprick of light that has its own heartbeat.

She has tried to break the bell jar three times.

The first time is an accident. While sweeping autumn leaves from her front room, the broom handle collides with the curved glass, sending it from the table to the floor. Beth's heart seems to pause as she watches the jar drop; she expects it to shatter into a thousand pieces and mourns its loss even before it is gone. Though the glass makes a familiar sound against the floor, it stays intact. The wheel inside doesn't even come loose from its moorings. A small blizzard of orange and flame leaves rise within the dome and from that moment, though unbroken, the tree continues to shed its bounty.

She expects the leaves to build up and eventually fill the jar, though they do not. She watches the bell jar, once for an entire afternoon, and she can see what happens. She can see the leaves slowly rot and if that is a skeleton barely visible beneath the tree's roots, she does not want to know. Let the leaves cover it. Better yet, let the thing break and become trash.

The second time, she throws the bell jar to the ground in an effort to make it just that. She is living alone in a lonesome place; the floors are stone yet worn smooth from the continued passage of her bare feet. Back and forth and back once more and she can no longer stand the tree with its damnable leaves. She hurls the jar into the stone and it simply rolls; rolls until it hits the wall. It remains whole.

Years pass. She does not count how many, but when the third attempt rolls around, she is running for her life. When people suspect what she can do—that she knows too much about their lives, that she can seemingly *control* some part of them—they allow fear to guide their actions. Driven from her home by women too enraged at the idea of what Beth knows of their husbands, Beth flees toward the low murmuring sound that has approached all day. Across this field and that, putting more distance between herself and those women, Beth finds herself at the edge of a railroad track.

She draws up before she stubs a toe against the ties, against the tracks, and only stands there, breathing, praying, listening. *Don't, don't, don't.* The longer she stands, the more she realizes she can no longer hear the women. Perhaps they have gone.

And then the train, blazing out of the night with its head-lamp, rushing past her so fast that her skirts fly up. The rush of wind through her tight brown curls is like laughter or fingers or some combination of both. Beth finds herself laughing and as the train passes her, she flings the bell jar at the caboose. The glass lands on the back porch and is carried off, deep into the night. Beth falls to her knees and presses her hands to the hot rail.

The little man finds her in the morning. She wakes, aware of a hand on her cheek and then her shoulder, and she opens her eyes to find a curious sight: the man can be no more than two feet tall, his face beautiful with gold dust and kohl, his lips turned into a bright red flower with green leaves that spread across his cheeks. On his shoulder perches a small monkey wearing an even smaller top-hat, and their eyes are the very same color, a color that Beth longs to drown in.

"You will need to collect your things," he tells her.

She can't go back there, can't risk those women, and the little man seems to know this without her saying a word. He takes her by the hand and tugs her up from the ground, walking with her along the railroad tracks. By noon, they reach the train.

The bell jar sits on the back porch of the caboose, looking none the worse for its adventure. The wheel is still upright and leaves continue to fall from the tree. Beth bursts into tears at the sight of it, watching the little man as he and an assortment of people from the train head off, toward town. Later, they return with her trunks.

The first time she watches them raise the great wheel, Beth feels like she will be sick. It is a long process for the workers, to dig the holes for the supports, to set the foundation and precisely place each panel that will hold a car. This, Eamonn tells her, is why they don't always raise the wheel. Only certain cities get the wheel and it's because they've paid extra for the time and risk.

Beth notes each little, worn red car that slots into place when the panels finally ring the axel like petals. She knows there will be twelve cars and that on windy days they will squeak, for so does the wheel within her jar. Eamonn sits beside her on the caboose's back step and they watch the process in silence, until Beth can watch no more. Still, she has nothing else to occupy her. Within this traveling circus she has no talent that might be put to use, not until Eamonn presses an orange into her palm and gives her the idea.

Her hands close around the orange, fingers seeking the rough skin as the wheel takes its first test spin. The wheel makes a horrific noise, all that metal and wood being forced to move, until it finds its rhythm and rolls easily within its frame.

"Sweet," Eamonn murmurs and leans into Beth's side.

She glances down at him and then to the orange. He may be talking about the wheel, but she's focused on the purpose he has placed within her hands. Sweet was not without bits of sour to counter it; Mother Night said everything has its beginning and so, too, its end.

Her first efforts are terrible, more tart than sweet, though the monkey Ichabod eats it without complaint. She sits on the back stoop to contemplate where she has gone wrong—with only the marmalade, for any truly complete list would run far into the future. She hears the wheel groan as it lifts another bunch of people into the night sky; she hears the fall of each leaf within the dome of the bell jar.

The idea of the jar draws her to her trunks, which have stayed locked all this time. She opens one, to look upon the jars that line its interior. They gleam as the light from the carnival hits them. All these things she has preserved: time and cities and small words that people have otherwise forgotten. Salvation. Hope. Mercy.

She is adding the laughter of a three-year-old child to a batch of orange marmalade when Jackson enters the caboose unannounced. Beth pauses mid-pour to stare at him, thinking he will tell her to get out, that he will smash every jar she's strewn about the caboose. But he instead shambles forward and nudges the jar up, preventing her from adding too much. Beth caps the jar while Jackson dips a long wooden spoon into the pot upon the stove. He tastes and then is smiling and laughing much as that three-year old had a hundred years before.

Beth closes her eyes and sees the thread of Jackson's life stretching far into the distance. When she looks closer, she can see the knots and deviations, the other threads he is tied to. Looking even closer, she can tell that she and he have skipped forward and back, with and without the train, and she sees the thing he cherishes most, the hand holding the cross which rests within his beloved locomotive, and she knows then—believes that if she can infuse such a memory into her marmalades, that though all things must end, she can make the in between bearable.

Beth does not know how long she has been with the circus train, nor does she care. Her days are spent helping people as she can. Rather than severing lines, she fuses them together for a little longer. But every fuse has its consequences, she knows. Everyone cannot go on forever and sometimes she must open jars she would rather not.

She kneels now before a jar wreathed in cobwebs, its label peeling and yellowed. The name that was once writ upon it is long gone, but it whispers in the back of Beth's mind. Her own name. The cork has been sealed with a thick coat of wax and she digs her nails into it, until she can pull the cork free. The air that filters out is stale but she breathes it in, accepting all she has denied herself.

The great wheel is not far from the caboose; though it is

night, crowds still revel amid the tents and booths. Children squeal and the scent of popcorn saturates the land. Beth's course is steady, a jar cradled within her hands. Her bare feet make no sound until fallen leaves begin to crunch underfoot.

There, near the base of the wheel, stands a tree. A few leaves yet cling to its thick branches and though they fly off under the cooling night air, they never seem to run out. At the base of the tree stands the young man, looking the way he did those many years ago when she startled him in a church grave-yard. He's dressed in the colors of the circus, though, for he works here, operating the great wheel. She knows he does not remember her, for she took that from him. (*And yet*, whispers that voice, *he does, for look, he is here and you are here.*)

A sob escapes Beth when she realizes what she has done—what she hasn't done—and she feels the weight of every second spent in this place pressing down upon her. She feels so heavy, she wonders how she will ever reach his side, but when she does, she's laughing, because he's looking at her as though he wants to say—

"No one comes here," he says, though the people around him contest those very words. The wheel slows behind him, and the people holler for him to fix it—make it go! His brow wrinkles.

Beth's laugh deepens and she offers the jar of pear butter she carries.

"You came here," she says, and when his hands close around the jar and he opens it, dipping two fingers in to taste the sweetness, the salvation, the wheel above them glides once more into smooth motion.

EVERY SEASON

2001, THE FOOTHILLS OF THE ROCKY MOUNTAINS

Every season, the circus comes.

Every season, Sam buys one jar of marmalade, always lemon, and leaves it on the kitchen table with its red checkerboard tablecloth. The sun slants through the jar, turning the marmalade to stained glass, a saffron puddle spreading to the edge of the table, dribbling over its edge. It never hits the floor, though Sam sometimes wishes it would, the same way he wishes for all things unspoken.

Every season, Harper sets the jar in the cupboard, unopened, where the shadows close over it and its brethren. Seven jars of lemon marmalade occupy the cupboard now, and Harper stares at them, unable to close the cupboard door, ink-stained fingers trembling on the handle. Harper didn't realize there were so many, and now they're an odd number, the rows no longer even and he can't stand it. He draws the seventh jar back out. He cradles it against his chest, small jar eclipsed by long fingers.

Harper puts the marmalade into his pack and leaves the house just as he always does, through the back door and toward the path cut through the field where, in the summer, the bees turn the air to vibrating confetti. Now, in late autumn, it is still but for the leaves that drip from the white-trunked birch, this a quieter celebration. It's all the same as it was, but for the weight of the marmalade in his pack, the way the bag makes a gentle *thump thump thump* against his back as he steps off the path and into the tall grasses that have begun to spin themselves into gold with the shortening of the days.

At the crest of the hill, he can see into the valley, the town nested between mountain and river, and today right where there had once been only an empty field, now a small eruption of tents and booths, the erection of a spinning wheel against the pumpkin sky. The breath Harper drags into his lungs is filled with the scents he knows and those he longs for. It would be so easy to walk down the hill and lose himself in the tents. Easy, but not simple, because there ...

He cannot let himself even think what might happen. He has chosen his path and it is not through the tents, but come evening, Sam presses.

"I think," Sam says, and Harper moves in his chair just enough that his foot hits the pack he dropped on the floor when he came in, his marmalade-laden pack, "I would like to go to the circus."

Sam brings dinner to the table and fills Harper's plate, but Harper hasn't moved, because that word, *circus*, feels lodged in his throat. Harper reaches for the glass of cold milk near his plate and takes a long drink; after a day spent working in a haze of smoke and profanity, it tastes like something of a miracle. "You're free to go."

Of course, Harper knows Sam has already been to the circus, because he bought the jar of marmalade. The travelling circus is the only place that has those jars, those flavors. Harper moves his foot so it's no longer touching his pack, and tries not to think about the six jars in the cupboard behind him.

Sam sinks into the chair closest to Harper's. The kitchen table is a square, but they've never sat at head and foot, always choosing to be diagonal to each other, as close as they can be. Harper covers Sam's hand with his own, long fingers closing gently around. It's like the first time Harper touched him all over again; in that smoky club, the gentle thump of music in the retreating distance as the world became them and only them.

"You have already been and you are free to go back," Harper says.

The protest dies between Sam's parted lips; Harper can't stop watching him, the way he opens his mouth to try again, tongue wetting his lips. Sam's cheeks are rough with stubble, cheekbones high, lashes still impossibly thick and dark, framing eyes that are bluer than blue tonight.

"I would like to go to the circus *with you*," Sam amends. "I think ..."

Harper knows what he thinks—what Sam *knows*. It is one thing to choose a path, but choosing one does not mean longing for another ceases. For Harper, choosing one path meant giving up all others, because the others were too—destructive is the word he decides on.

"I know you would." Harper leans in and his kiss for Sam lingers; he wants to say many things, but cannot, and even by the time they've done dishes, and put the kitchen back to rights, by the time they've curled into bed and turned out the lights, Harper still hasn't said any of them.

He waits for Sam's breathing to even out, for him to turn away in his sleep as he always does. Then, Harper slips from their bed, ties his robe around his body, and goes barefoot downstairs. His pack is where he left it, leaning against the kitchen table leg, and he grabs the straps, unlocking the back door a beat later. Barefoot through the moonlit autumn grass, he moves toward the old barn. There used to be horses and they've talked about getting others, but for now the stalls stand empty. Harper climbs to the loft where the memory of hay lingers and he sits on the splintered floor.

In the moonlight that cuts through the loft window, the marmalade jar gleams like gold in Harper's hands. It is a pleasant, cool weight, and he imagines himself opening it, breathing in the scent of the lemons. Not only lemons, he knows. His hands begin to tremble and he finds he cannot do it. Cannot break the seal and commit himself to the marmalade. Neither can he open it and leave it to rot, so he does not open it at all. He buries the jar in his pack and buries the pack in the shadows that clutter the loft corner.

Outside again, he does not linger under the moonlight. He comes back to bed, and if Sam notices the strands of hay upon the floor come morning, he does not say.

Harper's arms are loaded with groceries and he regrets not getting a handcart, especially when Maisie Walters bumps into him. The pickle jar slips from the crook of his arm and smashes into the tile flooring, glass and liquid and pickles everywhere. Maisie stares at the mess, astonishment transforming her ninety-year-old face.

"No worries, no worries."

It's Aidan's store and he's around the corner in a shot, calling for Silvia to grab the dustpan and mop as he holds Maisie away from the mess, knowing she means to kneel and get to cleaning. Aidan shoots a grin at Harper.

"No worries," he repeats.

There are forty-six places in the world named Paradise and this is one of them. Harper doesn't know if it actually is Paradise, but it is awfully close. The people are unfailingly kind and helpful, but he fears that would change if they understood his truest self. The idea of it all falling apart upsets him, but he can see the tops of the circus tents from the store windows; can see the tents from everywhere, it seems. If anyone knew—

He supposes it's funny. No one looks sideways at him and Sam, not even when they walk down the street with Sam's hand in Harper's back pocket. Even Maisie didn't blink when she found them kissing on the dock under clouds of fireworks at the 4th of July celebrations. Everyone thought it was nice they had each other. But if they knew the truth about—

"Here you go."

Aidan offers Harper an unbroken jar of pickles and Harper takes them with a nod. Once Aidan has rung up the order, bagging everything neatly, Harper realizes he doesn't have his pack. And his wallet's in his pack. His pack is in the dusty shadows of the barn loft, full of circus marmalade.

On account, Aidan says and shoos him out the door,

because Maisie can't leave well enough alone and she's trying to pick up the shards of glass that Silvia has already swept into the dust pan. The entire place smells of brine and when Harper steps outside, the scent of the circus is a sharp contrast.

Some years, he and Sam argue about whether it's a circus or a carnival. "Circus" implied a professional organization, didn't it, Sam wanted to know, but Harper wasn't sure. "Carnival" felt more true to what Harper remembered as a kid—what he tried not to remember. The way he'd step into a tent, the way the world would become only that close, warm space, the way the music had leaked into his bones. Didn't matter what the music was, it carried him away, until it was him and the music and nothing else, until his heart beat in rhythm with the drums, and he shed clothes and inhibitions until he was naked in the dirt, dancing as if his very life depended upon it.

"Hello."

Without realizing it, Harper finds he's walked to the edge of the circus. The carnival. Before him is the chain link fence and beyond that is a young girl, her face brown and glowing in the soft morning light. She's wrapped in a cape, hands bunched into the fabric to keep it closed. She's like a copper dandelion, all thin legs and body and an explosion of dark hair. A nimbus. At her side, there's a small man—not a child at all, but not even half the girl's height.

"Hello," Harper returns.

"We don't open till later, till it's dark and we look all properly lit up," she advises. The small man tugs at the hem of her cape, but she shushes him. "You can come back then."

Through the fence, she passes Harper a handful of bent tickets. They look water-stained and ancient, but Harper finds himself taking them. The paper is soft between his fingers, like if he rubbed his fingers back and forth, it would just come apart in small rolls. They are tickets for admission, not to just the grounds, but to specific tents for specific events. Drawings decorate some of the tickets: a monkey, a mummy, two winged bodies entwined into one.

"Oh. I—"

"Can see it in your bones," the girl says. "Circus folk."

The denial is on Harper's tongue, but she's already turned away, vanishing into the tents. Harper stares after her, swearing he saw wings in her wake, trailing lower than her cape, but she's gone and he isn't sure, and the circus stands there, beckoning. They weren't soft bird wings, but something of bone and leathered skin.

He turns his back on the circus and walks away. By the time he's home, the tickets are bent into the pocket of his jeans, but not forgotten. He can feel them pressing against his thigh as he unpacks the groceries. He doesn't mean to open the cupboard where the six jars of lemon marmalade sit, but he does, and he stares the way he's heard people stare into abysses. The marmalade stares back at him, daring him to—

"To what," he says to the empty kitchen. He lifts his chin, and thinks of the first time he was confronted by kids at school, the first time they called him *faggot, fag, fucker*. He remembers the crack of Phil's fist against his jaw and can taste the copper of blood against his tongue. But he remembers, too, the way the boy went down under Harper's own fist.

The marmalade is in his hand before he can reconsider again. The lid comes off easily beneath his anger-fueled fingers, and the scent of lemon is in his nose, bright and gold, and he can already feel himself going, though he hasn't dipped his fingers into the sweetness, hasn't allowed the memories to cross his tongue. The first time, all those years ago, it had been a mistake; they hadn't known what the marmalade could do, didn't know it contained everything a person needed. Everything they avoided. Jars full of time and memory, not just marmalade.

Harper digs two fingers into the marmalade, using them like a spoon to bring the tart sweetness to his mouth. His fingers sear lips and tongue because the marmalade contains the memory of his first time with Sam; Sam had speared him with two fingers this way, caressing lips and tongue, daring Harper to suck his fingers while the otherworldly voice of Holly Johnson pounded down through them, the world washing away in hues of fuchsia and emerald. The thumping bass drove them to the floor, further into each other. Harper falls to his knees now, the kitchen walls evaporating as he is pulled back in time.

The basement club is so small, and surely his eyeliner and hair occupy more of the sooty room than they should, but he doesn't care. Most of the people packed into the space have come to see him, have come to listen to the music that spins from his fingers. In his booth, Harper stands a god, Maybelline and Rimmel having crafted his face into something Venus herself would envy. His dark hair surrounds his ivory face like a cloud of ravens, so he's perched a small black bird at his crown; he found it in a bin at Goodwill, and maybe it was a white dove intended for a Christmas tree, but he's colored it black with Sharpies and wears it like a bonnet now, its beak burning silver under the club lights.

Excess pours from everyone in the room; quilted leather jackets, beaded jeans, the thump of solid boots and stiletto heels against the cracked checkerboard tile floor. The dim air is a haze of AquaNet, cigarette smoke, and Giorgio. That's when Sam walks in, on the arm of a man Harper will always call Steve McQueen; he's got that rugged, devil-may-care kind of face, whereas Sam is all libertine highwayman Adam Ant, sharp face drawn sharper with pencil and lipstick. The gold ball buttons on his white vest spark like fire as the club lights wash over him, his belt slanting low across his hips.

Harper hungers, but Sam is swallowed by the crowd, and the night pounds on, vinyl tracks flowing one into the other under Harper's swift fingers. He loves finding the perfect juxtaposition of songs, of notes; loves rolling one song into the other without pause. In another time, he thinks he might've been a minstrel, might have written and composed, but here, this is as close as he'll get and he's fine with that.

The crowd never stops moving, not even when Harper's set becomes Wilde's, the disco-pop awash in heavy metals as the new tide rolls in. Harper squeezes through the crowd and up the stairs, hands ghosting over his shoulders, back, and legs as he climbs his way back into the street. It's winter, and he steams in the cold air, T-shirt sleeves raked up to his shoulders, digging his hands into his hair when Sam finds him. Harper exhales and it's all fog between them, until it's just the slanting streetlight, turning Sam's buttons vaguely orange.

"That was you?" Sam asks. "The music."

The black bird drops out of Harper's hair, a dry rustle against the street. "That was me."

The music still pounds through Harper's veins and he knows it's telling him to close the distance between himself and Sam; he wants to kiss that painted mouth and know what Sam was drinking (vodka, his far-away-mind knows). But Steve McQueen comes up behind Sam a breath later, and they move down the street, toward cars parked in shadow.

Harper turns to watch them go. Turns, mostly, to watch Sam's backside in retreat, black leather still hugging him after all that dancing. Sam passes through an angle of streetlight and turns, too, and Harper is blinded for a moment by all those gold buttons. He raises a hand as if to ward them off, but his fingers are sticky with marmalade, and he's on the floor of a kitchen thirty years distant from that winter street.

Harper leaves the house before sunrise. If Sam smelled the marmalade the night before, he didn't mention it. Harper didn't finish the jar, but swallowed half of it, and it terrifies him. The knowledge that he could so easily devour every jar in the cabinet without blinking. It's not just memories of him and Sam in the jars; it could be memories of *anything*. He doesn't know how the circus does it, doesn't know who makes the marmalade, but he's known enough to avoid the circus after their first visit. No one should know the things those jars hold; no one should have access to a man's mind like that.

Still, he wants to know.

The tattoo parlor sits on the corner of the town's oldest block; the building used to house a drugstore and soda shop. Harper found the original sign in the store room when they were setting up, so it hangs over the front desk. *Paradise Drugs* it reads in patina-spotted chrome, and everyone who comes in still has a good laugh over it. One man had it tattooed across his shoulders, bits of the sign flaking down his back in inky splotches. The parlor is quiet now and Harper's a good six hours early; he's only got one appointment on the books: a woman named Delilah.

He sits in the darkness a long time, unable to shake the memory of the club. The memory of Sam. When Kelly lets him know Delilah is ready, Harper can't quite believe it's already noon, because in his mind he was back at the club. Did Kelly talk to him when she arrived? Harper doesn't remember, but comes out to greet Delilah. Only, he freezes at the sight of her because she's from the circus.

The shop gets all kinds; even in a tiny place like Paradise, the unusual tend to collect, so Harper doesn't typically bat an eye at the people who come in. But Delilah is like an old memory. She is something ancient, something Harper recognizes and responds to. Her body is generous in every place, be it curved or hollowed, her sharp face punctuated by a glorious beard that lays braided in a thousand plaits between her breasts. Some might say the beard was only brown, but Harper recognizes all the colors inside: the copper, the mahogany, the glimmers of gold and even silver. Harper wants nothing more than to press his cheek against her warm, bare belly in a field of lavender and listen to every sound she makes.

"Suppose I surprised you," Delilah says as she sinks into Harper's chair at his station.

"Surprised me," Harper repeats. He feels incapable of speech and turns to pull his gloves on. The ink sits sealed on its tray, the machine all ready to go, but he feels disconnected from the moment entirely.

She doesn't want anything complicated; a trail of black stars down her inner left arm, she said on the phone, so Harper set his station accordingly. But once she sits in the chair, everything radiates complication. She looks like a queen, his chair a throne. She is a beacon to him, the way the girl was at the fence. A portal into a world he turned his back on.

"Gabrielle said she saw you—a man with music in him. At the fence. Gave you tickets."

Delilah wants free-hand stars from wrist to elbow, so Harper didn't make a stencil. He strokes her arm clean with rubbing alcohol, veins running under her skin like ribbons. He doesn't want to think about the girl at the fence or how that girl talked to this woman, how that girl called him a man with music in him. Harper picks up his tattoo iron and its weight in his hand is a comfort.

"Can smell the marmalade on you," Delilah says when the needles touch her skin for the first time.

Harper doesn't flinch, least not in his hands. He doesn"t look up at her either, focused on inking a star into her flesh. He fills some of them, until they are wholly black, blotting out her brown skin; others he leaves open, especially the star he places in the hollow of her elbow, where the ribbons of her veins coalesce.

"Have you tasted it?" Harper asks, blotting blood from his work. Do the circus people eat the marmalade? Do they feast every night? He sets to making another star.

"Can taste it on you now."

Harper flinches so violently, the tattoo iron skitters from his hand, but Delilah catches it before it can hit the floor. She thumbs it into silence, its soft buzzing no more, and they sit there under the bright lights, listening to each other breathe. Harper doesn't want to meet her eyes, and also wants it more than he's wanted anything. He drags his glance up her beard, past her mouth, to her eyes. They are yellow in the shadows, yellow like the marmalade.

"I'm not sure," Delilah says, "if you understand it and are afraid, or if you don't understand it and that's what drives the fear."

He takes in a deep breath, nostrils flaring.

"So it's the former," Delilah says. She holds the iron in her hand the way she might an egg, fingers curled around it. The needles drool ink down her fingers as the machine exhales. "You know that music never leaves your bones. The need to dance and frolic the way we all used to. They believe it was only women, but what's a woman after all."

Delilah sets the machine aside and reaches for Harper's hand, drawing it abruptly between her legs, where she's as stiff as Harper is every morning he wakes.

"Same as a man. Skin and bone and needs that can't be explained. Your man knows, too—doesn't he? Brings you those jars—I seen him come to the tents. Bringing the marmalade to you like he's begging you to let go, because didn't you once, under the olive trees at the edge of the world, with the leopards and the snakes. Naked in the dirt once you pulled your fawn skin off. Washed yourself clean in wine." There is only a breath of silence. "Is it the denial that pleases you?"

"Madness isn't—" Harper struggles to find the right word. He realizes Delilah has let go of his hand and his hand still rests between her legs. He withdraws, his hand fingerprinted in the same ink she wears.

"Is it madness to be who you are?"

"I wanted—" Harper realizes how hollow this want sounds, leaning as he is on Delilah's plump thighs. "A normal life."

"Who decides normal? Moon's full tonight."

Harper turns the question over in his head, even after Delilah leaves the shop. He bandaged her arm, and told her about aftercare, but he thinks the tattoos will heal overnight, after she's danced in the moonlight. The memory of dancing under a full moon is so sharp it brings tears to Harper's eyes. He can taste the night air on his lips and remember what it was to lose himself to the music, to the heavenly fires. Can remember what it was to rim his eyes in black liner, to wash his lips in crimson and pink.

He wonders at the message that comes from Sam a while later; Sam's working late, won't be home for dinner and Harper shouldn't wait up. A whole night before him and it's like a thorn in his heart. When he leaves the shop, he stands on the stoop, unsure of where to go. He looks back into the shop where Kelly and Manfred are cleaning up, where Silas is finishing some fill work, and Harper almost goes back inside.

A whole night before him and the scent of the circus snakes

through Paradise, popped corn and burnt sugar. He's walking that way before he decides otherwise, telling himself a look never hurt anyone. Why he stood at that fence and was fine, just fine, not remotely tempted.

Harper knows he used to be a better liar, because every step closer to the circus makes him feel like he's hip-deep in a sea of temptation. It's not the little winged girl who stands at the entry, but a gentleman Harper has never seen yet feels he knows. The man, seemingly bent and gnarled with age and pain, still bears himself as the owner of the revels, the man in charge, the one who knows when he's well and truly caught a wriggling fish.

"Ah, music," he says, and waves Harper's money and tickets away. "You are kin. Enter and be free."

A denial sits on Harper's lips, but he steps past the man and spits all denials into the dirt. Harper enters the circus, eyes and skin awash in the globe lights that stretch from tent to tent, the striped fabrics making walkways through the endless sights. Its cotton candy here, and butter and oil, but if he breathes deeply enough, he smells the darker things too: the perfumes, the shaken silks, the lust that clogs each and every show. Somewhere deeper in the tents, there is a drum, and the vibration pounds through the ground, up into Harper's legs.

It isn't fear that floods him now, but desire. It used to be, he couldn't listen to the radio without losing some part of himself to the music and the dance. Couldn't turn on the television for fear it would carry him away, and to this day he and Sam don't own one. The jingle of a commercial, the theme of a popular show, it all felt too perilously close to the edge of a crevasse Harper didn't want to fall over. He learned to control it—there was music every place in the world, and if he meant to have a normal life—

Who decides normal?

—he couldn't ignore the world.

But here, the drums are more primal, as they are meant to be. It is a rhythm rooted in the past, in the memories he has tried so long to deny.

When Harper finds them—his people, those he recognizes without blinking—they encircle a roaring fire. The women dance, not caring who sees, their bodies in ceaseless motion with the flames. Some hold great staves of flowering fennel, and others wands covered with ivy and topped with cones, but all are decked in ribbons, be they worn in their hair or around their ankles. Some have wrapped their waists; some have tied their arms. Some of the women go naked around the flames, and others wear animal skins; some wear long Grecian tunics, in the colors of blood and sky.

The sight of them is no less than a punch in Harper's gut. He reaches a hand out, to steady himself on the nearest thing. He thinks it will be a tent pole, but his fingers enclose a firm, fleshy arm, and he looks up, startled at the face that looks back. Neither male nor female, human nor animal, it is a face he knows, a body he ran beside long, long ago, when the world was still soft and forming. His breath is stolen when he looks into the amber eyes, when the clawed hand takes his own and pulls him toward the fire.

Harper wants to say no—his tongue presses to the back of his teeth because he *means* to say it, but the word evaporates under the heat of the flames, and is washed away entirely when he drinks from the goblet of crimson wine making the rounds. The outside world is so distant, it may as well not exist; in this place, there is the fire and there is the music. Harper gives himself up to both, because this way lies the person he remembers, the woman who moves without hesitation or doubt, the woman who is wiser than he will ever be.

In the old stories it was said that no fire could burn a

maenad, that no iron weapon could injure them. Harper walks through the crackling fire, flames licking his legs and chest, and emerges unburnt. He reaches the other side of the flames naked and steaming, feeling cleansed and whole. Women drape him in linens of ruby and gilt that smell of cloves. A snake twines around his waist, and fennel flowers sprinkle his hair.

Harper falls to his knees in the dirt, gasping for breath though he's breathing better than he has in years. His body responds to this world in a way he has tried to forget; these women are him; he is these women. His fingers claw at the dirt as he tries to stand and milk bubbles up from the ground under his touch. It floods the ground, surging around the dancers' feet, until they're stomping in it, celebratory, milky and muddy both.

The night is eternal and leopards prowl the shadows. At some point, Harper sleeps, but it does not feel like rest, for the music thrums through his body the entire time. He is aware of the way his heart matches the rhythm of the drum, aware of the way Delilah's fingers on his ankle match the twitter of a flute. It isn't sex, though it could be, the twining of a thousand bodies in this place; it's something deeper, more primal. It is a thousand bodies in synchronous motion, each knowing the impetus of the other, each understanding there is no deceleration—there is only acceleration in an opposite direction, because the dance does not stop. If they were birds, they would be a murmuration in the sky, a thousand separate pieces moving as one.

It is early when he returns home—or maybe late, Harper isn't sure. He sits on the porch steps, watching the sun begin to color the sky, and feels as though he has never truly seen the colors before this moment. He knows their names, can list them as gold and peach and sienna in the clouded shadows, but they reach beyond their names today. They evoke the colors of the fire that burned him clean, the fire that made him whole.

The linens haven't evaporated, nor the chains of gold at his neck, nor the hoops of silver in his ears. He is not Cinderella, whose finery evaporates at midnight. He wears rings that belong to other dancers, and is streaked with soot and dirt, makeup and perfume, when Sam finds him still sitting on the porch steps. Harper thinks to explain, but the words stick in his throat. Sam knows, surely Sam knows, because he left the marmalade, all those jars nestled in the cupboard, a waiting invitation. It's like a fist in Harper's throat. He can't speak.

Sam kisses Harper before Harper can muster anything, licking soot and lipstick from him in equal measure. Sam's teeth catch Harper's lower lip and it is as primal, if not more so, than the night before. Something (the bees that would turn the air to confetti, he thinks) inside Harper responds to Sam the way he did to the fire, to the dancing. He knows Sam's tongue would wash him clean like the fire did, hot but not burning, until his true self was exposed.

But this idea is as revolting as it is compelling. The longing inside Harper nauseates him, and he pushes Sam away, staggering down the porch steps. He tries to catch a breath and waves Sam away when Sam would follow, but Sam doesn't listen. Sam lunges for him, enclosing Harper's wrist in his iron hold. Harper tries to wrench away, but Sam will not let go, and so Harper comes to face him again. Their eyes are furious, breaths hard.

"Don't you know," Sam says, his voice rough and breaking. "It's *you*. It doesn't matter what the world sees—it's you as you are that compels me. I would have you however you are."

It is this that terrifies Harper. Sam's hand eases just a bit and Harper takes the opening; he pulls himself free and steps back, earrings and chains surrounding him with their own music. He sounds like bells, brief church bells ringing over clear hills. And Sam—oh, Sam. Sam looks as though he's been punched, his beautiful face smeared with tears. Once, there would have been makeup running down his cheeks, too. How they have changed, Harper thinks. And yet, how they have not.

———

Who decides normal?

Harper doesn't know, but decides to leave the house just as he always does, through the back door and toward the path cut through the field where, in the summer, the bees hold court. Their boxes stand quiet now and it is still but for the leaves dropping when the air moves through. Harper feels as hollow as the old log he sits on, dry on the outside, but filled with dark, rotting life even so. He sets his pack near his foot and does not look at it; he stares toward the ridge of the hill, beyond which sits the city and now the circus. One does not know who he truly is; the other knows and would revel in it the way he longs to.

He means to leave entirely, to run as he has always run, but finds himself reaching for his pack. It holds six and a half jars of marmalade and the sun glints off the small rounded jars as he opens the flap. Each jar and lid are the same and he thinks that surely by now time will have made the oldest of them inedible, but he opens one at random, and it smells as sweet as the newest Sam brought him.

The marmalade is firm under his fingers, but he scoops out a taste, and then another. He does not know how it is possible, but the marmalade carries him backward in time, and he's standing at his mother's bathroom vanity. The bathroom is tiled in pink and black, a realm his father has never entered. Harper doesn't know if that's a rule and doesn't care. His mother's coffee and toast sit nearby and he takes a big bite of the marmalade slathered toast before looking over her cosmetics.

Once he's painted his face on, Harper exhales. He doesn't

know what it is about the face that looks at him from the mirror, but it is better. It is more ... him.

Barefoot, he walks to his father's den, a room that sits dark amid the rest of the house. Usually, Harper only comes in here when he's in trouble, but when he's in trouble, it's the vast shelves of vinyl albums that cover the far wall which interest him. He has heard the music only through the closed den door; only through the floorboards, for his bedroom sits above the den.

Barefoot, Harper crosses the wood floor and stands before the shelves, and tells himself it is not *him* who is touching the spines of the albums with his carefully painted nails. It is not his mouth pursing in delight, but someone else's. Here, he is not Timothy Spencer.

His fingers rake over the albums and he thinks about a harp, about a harper, and this is what he calls himself from this moment on. It is Harper who slides a pristine album free, its paper liner whispering as the vinyl disk comes free. It is Harper who sets the needle into the groove, and Harper who loses himself in the music, who loses himself to the point his mother finds him passed out on the den floor that afternoon, the record skipping in its final track.

Oh, if your father knew ...

His mother's whisper is a soft warning of all there is to hide. Harper knows it's not the trespass she worries about, but everything else. The lipstick, the nail polish, the sweet marmalade in his mouth. She helps Harper clean up, until all appears as it should be, vinyl and son never disturbed. But all through dinner, Harper thinks about the music, and the way it filled his bones; the way he allowed it to carry him far away from the life he knows and into another. A life where bodies gave themselves up to the dance, a life where the dance was all. He knew that life once; he's sure of it.

His father died before he could know any of it, albums sold before Harper could find the voice to say he wanted them. As Harper walks back to the house, the day fading into evening already, he wonders if that's part of the reason he's chased the music so long—to reclaim what he let slip away through silence and inaction. It is this thought that grips him as he comes into the kitchen where Sam sits at the table.

Harper sets his pack beside the door and crosses the room to Sam, where he kneels and folds Sam's hands into his own. Sam draws in a breath and does not exhale.

"I would like to go to the circus," Harper says. And in the silence that follows adds, "With you."

Harper and Sam walk through the circus gates together, the round bulb lights shining like stars that have come down from the heavens, close enough to touch. Within Harper's fingers, they crackle. The air itself is electric and the barker's welcome feels like a homecoming, though Harper never called this place home, not really. Not yet.

Under the circus lights, Harper watches as Sam is transformed; as the quiet mask he wore for the outside world is stripped away, and he becomes what he has always been, a sharp-cheeked libertine in a long dark coat, ready to carry Harper into the night. Harper can see himself in Sam's eyes, can see the way he has changed. No longer Timothy Spencer, but well and truly Harper who wears ribbons in his hair, and a long flowing gown that is the color of a solstice midnight sky.

Sam takes Harper's hands and kisses them and—

Harper wants to go slow, but cannot. He lassoes his love's libertine spirit and pulls Sam into the circus depths, into the mounting frenzy of the maenad camp within. In the bonfire-blurred air, he sees the woman who makes the marmalade, and watches her dance among the maenads, though she is not one of them. Harper does not yet know what she is, but her skin shimmers with a thousand thousand stories she has yet to tell. Stories that are not her own, stories her sisters have woven and she has cut when they are at their end. The way she cuts citrus rinds. He feels his life sliding through the hands of her and her sisters, as if he, too, is being peeled. He can see in her the end of every thing and it is as compelling as it is terrifying.

He spins away from her still face, as if he can stop the march of time. With Sam in his arms, and the dirt between his toes, the fire blinding him to all else, he thinks perhaps he can. There is only the dance, only the weight of Sam against him as they orbit the fire.

Every season, the circus comes. The train winds its way across the land, into and out of lives as it will, disregarding every clock and calendar, every mountain and every ocean. The circus goes where it will.

Every season, Sam buys one jar of marmalade—sometimes lemon and sometimes orange—and brings it to Harper. They take turns devouring it within the circus train car they share. With fingers and spoons, they eat until the jar is empty. Until they have remembered what it is to live, what it is to truly be alive.

INLAND TERRITORY, STRAY ITALIAN GREYHOUND

THE END OF THE WORLD

At the end of all things, there remains this: the battered circus train moving through a smudged charcoal world. This train—those who know the train best call her *she, her, sister*—serpentine and sure, knows that at the end of these rails—even if broken—there will be something, someone, somewhere. The train says so.

High above in the clouded sky that is never broken with sunlight, Gabrielle circles. She is a woman, she is a brown bat, she is both things at once. She once could not fly, only gliding where the air would take her, but now she has made lovers of the wind, the ragged clouds. In the remains of this ruined world, her small and once-broken body gleams amber, beautiful and strange, like and unlike every other creature on the train below.

The train crossed low tracks just that morning, tracks submerged in salt waters that were thick with algae bloom; the train said it could be done—the train did not lie, for the silver sisters who knew metal better than any threaded their fingers beneath the toxic waters, to heat the tracks to burn the algae and despite the stench (oh, they had smelled worse), the train plowed through. The water fanned out, gray with the dead, blue with sorrow, edged in foam that tries to be white.

More waters now and Gabrielle circles down and down, plunging through clouds the way she loves best: headfirst, eyes wide. She bullets downward, red tide spilling over the track they follow. Within the waters stands a dog, a skeletal greyhound who is as thin as ribs and as gray as hope. The dog stands up to her bony knees in the filth and shakes, small ripples moving ever outward from the bones. Gabrielle touches down on the roof of the still train and while others clear the red tide, she watches only this dog. She clicks her tongue and those proud ears perk forward.

"Dogness," she says, her own voice gone strange to her in this wet air.

The dog does not move, so Gabrielle does. She falls with grace from the roof, wings unfurled to slow her toes when they touch and break the water's surface. The dog steps backward, as if they are dancing, and Gabrielle approaches slowly, wings tucked, not daring, not hoping, until the dog bends her head, dips her cold and shaking skull into Gabrielle's cold and shaking hand.

And so onto the train comes the dog—the dog who is called Drowned, who is called Lake and Tremble, who is called a thing Gabrielle never dared hope for (*Future, Running, Reaching*), but the train always knew—there would be something here, a someone, a somewhere.

So onward they go, where track and train lead, at the end of all things, through a smudged charcoal world.

THE END

ACKNOWLEDGMENTS

In the late 1990s, I spent a lot of time writing in online RPGs, many of them bulletin board-based, or even email-based. Essentially, we were writing short stories that just lasted for a year or longer. We built worlds. We made maps. We developed characters I remember to this day. We made mix tapes. We drew art. We wrote, and we wrote, and we wrote.

These friends would inspire me to try new things with my writing—I knew nothing, had published nothing, but I wanted to publish very much. Every segment of story that was posted made me wonder how I could do that thing in my own fiction. And then, everything changed.

Someone new joined a game we had going, and added a layer that we absolutely had never had before. Grit, oil, *voice*. Reading posts from this player was astonishing, because I'd never been drawn into a story quite this way before. Prior to his arrival, our characters absolutely occupied all the posh uptown spaces we knew we'd never enter; this new player introduced gritty downtown characters who transformed the game and challenged my writing.

I wrote "Vanishing Act" as a challenge to myself, and a tribute to that new player—to he who became a friend (and later introduced me to *Cowboy Bebop*, which was its own influence!). Jackson's Unreal Circus and Mobile Marmalade would not exist without Jay Knioum, who brought his A-game and dared me to bring mine. Neither would this universe exist without Ellen Datlow, who read "Vanishing Act" and bought it for *SciFiction*. Selling the story gave me the courage to write more stories.

Editor Scott H. Andrews of *Beneath Ceaseless Skies* is also to blame—my circus stories seem to have found a natural home in his magazine. A.C. Wise must also be acknowledged, for she has been a tireless supporter of this world and its adventures for years. Writing can be so solitary, and knowing that someone wants to read the next story is *huge*.

Editors Jason Sizemore and Lesley Conner also harbor some share of the blame, because when I finally pushed myself to write Jackson's origin story (*The Kraken Sea*), they had the audacity to publish it. And now here they are, publishing a collection!

My travelling circus stories have come to be vastly important to me. Much as I wanted to pay tribute to a friend's use of voice in the first story, other stories came to be small tributes to other friends, to loves, and losses, things I wished I had said, and things I wish I could do. These stories are tiny glimpses of things readers may never fully understand, but they are tiny glimpses into my heart.

E. Catherine Tobler
March 2020, Colorado

ABOUT THE AUTHOR

E. Catherine Tobler has never run away with the circus, but there's still time. Among others, her short fiction has appeared in *Clarkesworld*, *Lightspeed*, and *Apex Magazine*. She edited the World Fantasy and Hugo-finalist *Shimmer Magazine*, and co-edited the World Fantasy Award finalist anthology, *Sword & Sonnet*. You can find her website at www.ecatherine.com.

 twitter.com/ecthetwit